Truphena
Student Nurse

PHOENIX YOUNG READERS SERIES

1. The Lonely Black Pig — Anne Matindi
2. The Sun and the Wind — Anne Matindi
3. The Pet Snake — Dickson Mukunyi
4. The Greedy Host — J. K Njoroge
5. The Speck of Gold — Cynthia Hunter
6. The Peacock and the Snake — Elijah K. Soi
7. Cock and Lion — Kalondu Kyendo
8. Beautiful Nyakio — Frederick Ndungu
9. Children of the Forest — Joel Makumi
10. Mzee Nyachote — Roeland Japuojo
11. The Fly Whisk — Stephen Gichuru
12. The Talking Devil — Leo Odera Omolo
1 3. The Feather in the Lake — Joel Makumi
14. Give the Devil his Due — W. K. Boruett
15. Inspector Rajabu Investigates — F. Kawegere
16. The Powerful Magician — Daniel Irungu
17. End of the Beginning — Joel Makumi
18. Onyango's Triumph — Leo Odera Omolo
1 9. Tales of Wamugumo — Peter N. Kuguru
20. The Girl who Couldn't Keep a Secret — Clare Omanga
21. Wake Up and Open Your Eyes — Edward Muhire
22. The Proud Ostrich — J. K. Njoroge
23. Njogu The Prophet — JamlickMutua
24. Travels of a Raindrop — David Ng'osos
25. The Adventures of Thiga — C. M. Mureithi
26. Pamela the Probation Officer — Cynthia Hunter
27. Anna the Air Hostess — Cynthia Hunter
28. The Circle of Revenge — David Mwaurah
29. Town Tricksters — David Mwaurah
30. Truphena Student Nurse — Cynthia Hunter
31. Truphena City Nurse — Cynthia Hunter
32. Captured by Raiders — Benjamin Wegesa
33. The Great Siege of Fort Jesus — Valerie Cuthbert

and more.........and many more

Truphena
Student Nurse

Cynthia E. Hunter

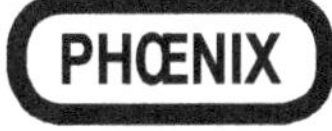

PHOENIX PUBLISHERS, NAIROBI

First published in 1966
First Phoenix edition published in 1988
This edition reset to B6 format
and published in 1989 by
Phoenix Publishers Ltd.,
Mellow Heights, Ngara Road.
P.O Box 30474-00100,
Nairobi.

ISBN 9966 47 096 4

Reprinted in 1991,1993, 1995,1997,1999, 2002, 2003, 2006, 2008, 2010, 2011, 2012, 2014, 2016, 2019

Printed by
Modern Lithographic (K) Limited
P.O. Box 52810 - 00200,
Nairobi,
Kenya.

DEDICATION

To my daughters, Christine and Barby

Although the characters in this book are not intended to resemble any known person, living or dead, the author hopes to have portrayed something of the spirit of a noble profession.

The author wishes to acknowledge the help of students, nurses and doctors and the Flying Doctor Services.

Contents

Prologue 1

1. Truphena Arrives at the Hospital................................ 7

2. On Tour with Matron 18

3. Work and Play 29

4   On the Wards 38

5. The Accident.. 48

6. The Surprise 58

7. Night Duty.. 67

8. A Wonderful Adventure...................................76

9. Finals 86

10. The Decision 95

Glossary of Technical Terms 101

Prologue

Truphena lay on her narrow bed not daring to move in case she woke her small brother, Benaiah, who was sleeping beside her. She could feel his warm body and hear his soft breathing. The light from the full moon shone through the window. She could see Benaiah's face which was turned towards her. His little arms were stretched above his head and in one hand he clutched Truphena's yellow headscarf. Suddenly he opened his eyes wide and sat up with a cry.

"It's all right, darling, you are safe at home and quite well now," whispered Truphena.

Benaiah gave a sleepy smile when he heard his sister's voice and sank back on the bed. Truphena put her arms round him and soon he was sleeping peacefully; but she was unable to sleep because her mind was too full of the nightmare of the last few days.

* * *

It was holiday time and Truphena had been left in charge of her younger brothers and sisters. Her mother and father had gone to visit some friends to see their new baby. Rebecca and Penina were playing around outside the hut and Juma and Mulimu were looking after the cows; Benaiah, always her favourite, was toddling after Truphena as she went about her work.

Suddenly, Benaiah started to cry and said that his leg hurt. The day before, he had scratched it on a tin which had carelessly been left lying around; it had only been a small scratch and no one had taken much notice at the time. Now Truphena saw that the leg looked swollen so she fetched a mat and told Benaiah to lie down beside her whilst she started to make the midday meal.

Benaiah stopped crying and seemed to be asleep. The only sounds to be heard were the children's laughter from outside the hut and the occasional lowing of the new cow which had not yet become used to its surroundings. Then Benaiah started to make sucking noises as he breathed. Truphena looked at him and saw his eyes were open. She called his name, but he seemed neither to see nor hear her. His breathing became louder and he looked stretched and stiff. She called his name again. Benaiah shuddered but gave no answer. Truphena knew he was very ill.

There was a hospital at Lakimu, but that was a long way off; Truphena had no idea how far. She remembered that once a large white car, with a red cross on the side, had come from the hospital to fetch her father's sister, who had been very sick. Everyone had thought that her aunt would die, but two weeks later the same car had brought the old lady back again, quite well.

"If I can take Benaiah to the hospital, he will get better," she said to herself. She called Juma and told him to go on stirring the food until it was ready and then to call the others and have their meal. She explained that she must take Banaiah to the hospital and when Juma saw how ill the child was, he agreed.

Truphena walked down the road with Benaiah stiff and heavy in her arms. After a time, she felt hot and thirsty; her arms ached and her mouth was so dry that her tongue felt swollen. A few people passed; some looked at Benaiah and shook their heads. "I must get him there, I must, I must," she kept saying to herself. "If I get to the hospital, I know the doctor will save him."

She did not know how far she had gone when a young man came up to her, wheeling a cart. "Where are you going?" he asked Truphena.

"I am taking my brother to the hospital and I must get there quickly," answered Truphena, stumbling over a hole in the road.

"I have just been to the market and sold my bananas," said the young man. "You can put your brother in my cart and I'll wheel him to the hospital."

Truphena gratefully laid Benaiah gently in the cart and walked along beside him. She swung her arms, as she walked, to get rid of the pain, but her feet were sore and she was still very thirsty.

"Where have you come from?" asked the young man.

"I have come from Maronga," answered Truphena.

"That is ten kilometres away. How could you have walked so far, carrying this heavy child?"

"See, he is very ill," said Truphena, "but if I take him to the hospital, he will get better. How much further is it?"

"About another two kilometres," answered the young man.

They walked on in silence. Clouds appeared in the sky, lessening the fierce heat of the sun, but Truphena hoped that it would not rain before she had come to the end of her journey.

At last they came to a large, white building. "There is the hospital," said the young man. "You go along that path to the building and you will see a lot of people waiting. That is called the 'Out-Patients'. You wait there and someone will come to see what you want. Good-bye and good luck!"

"Good-bye and thank you," gasped Truphena, as she picked up Benaiah in her arms and staggered along the path towards the hospital. She pushed her way through the crowd and went up to a man in a white coat who had something dangling round his neck. He looked important and she thought that he must be the doctor. A girl in a pink dress and a white cap and apron came up to her and began to tell her to go the end of the line of people, but an older woman, in a blue dress, who had seen Truphena struggling up the path came and looked at Benaiah. She called the doctor in a serious voice.

After that Truphena could not remember what had happened. She found herself on a hard bench and the girl in the pink dress was standing over her. When the girl saw Truphena open her eyes, she handed her a glass of water. Truphena drank gratefully. "What have you done with Benaiah?" she called out.

At that moment, the doctor came over and asked how old she was.

"I am twelve," she answered.

"And how old is your brother?"

"He is about a year and a half."

"You have done well to bring him here," said the doctor. "He is very ill indeed; we do not know yet if we can save him, but we shall do everything we can. If he lives until morning, all will be well. How far have you come?"

Truphena told him. "You cannot go home now," said the doctor. "Nurse will arrange somewhere for you to spend the night. In the morning you may come and see how your brother is; you must understand, we can only do our best."

Until that moment, Truphena had had no thought of tears, but hearing the doctor's kindly voice, her self-control gave way and tears streamed down her face. "Let her cry," said the doctor, as the nurse led her away. "It is better that way."

Next morning the nurse took Truphena over to the hospital. When she saw the doctor, she hardly dared ask the only question that was in her mind.

Truphena picked up Benaiah in her arms and staggered along the path towards the hospital.

"Your brother will live," he said quietly. "You may see him for a few moments and then our driver will take you to about a mile from your home; he has to take the ambulance to fetch a patient from Mwihaka. Tell your mother to come in five days time."

* * * *

That morning Truphena had gone on the bus with her mother to fetch Benaiah. He was looking thin, but was quite well.

"Thank you, doctor, for saving my son," her mother had said.

"If your daughter had not brought him to hospital in time, I could not have saved him," replied the doctor. "And you must thank nurse Perlita. She stayed by his side and carried out all my instructions until he was out of danger. A doctor's treatment is often useless without good nursing. The illness your son had is called tetanus," continued the doctor. "It comes through dirt getting into a cut. The cut may be so tiny that you do not even notice it. We can give an inoculation that will prevent this happening. I suggest that you bring all your family here next week to have this done."

Truphena looked up and saw that Benaiah had his arms round the neck of a smiling nurse.

* * * *

All this passed again through Truphena's mind as she lay there with Benaiah in her arms. Suddenly a tremendous thought came to her.

"When I am old enough, I shall be a nurse," she said to herself.

She sighed contentedly and fell asleep.

Chapter 1

Truphena Arrives at the Hospital

As the bus jogged along the bumpy road towards the hospital, Truphena thought of the day when she had carried Benaiah in her arms along the same road. She realized that it had been the turning point in her life. The decision to become a nurse had never changed and today she was to begin her training.

She was now an attractive girl of seventeen. She had passed her school leaving examination and had been called for an interview at the hospital.

"I can only choose fourteen people out of over a hundred who have applied to come," she remembered Matron saying to her. She had waited anxiously for a whole month until the letter arrived telling her to report the following week. Now she was on her way to a new life.

A few miles from the hospital, a young man waved the bus to a halt and sprang inside. Truphena thought she had seen him before; he looked at her but showed no signs of recognition. Suddenly she realized that he was the young man who had pushed Benaiah to the hospital in his wheelbarrow.

The bus stopped at the hospital gates and Truphena picked up her small suitcase and stepped off. As she walked up the path, she noticed that the young man was following her. She passed the 'Out-Patients' and saw a lady in a white coat bending over one of the children. "She must be a special kind of nurse," thought Truphena. Further on, she saw a door marked 'Matron'.

She knocked timidly. "Come in!" said a pleasant voice. Truphena opened the door and went inside. Miss Robinson, the Matron, was sitting at her desk. She had on a dark blue dress with a crisp, white collar and cuffs. Her short, grey hair curled round the ends of her stiff, white cap. Her strong hands lay still on her lap. On the desk was a clean sheet of blotting paper, a notebook and various pens and pencils. Neat piles of letters and papers were stacked in wire trays.

"Good afternoon," said the Matron, "you have arrived in good time. Did you meet anyone elese who was coming here on your journey?"

At that moment there was a loud knock on the door. Truphena heard some whispering outside. "Come in," called Matron. The door opened and in walked four girls and the young man whom Truphena had seen on the way.

"Tell me your names," said Matron, "and I shall know who is still to come."

As they gave their names, Matron ticked them off on a list in front of her.

"There is one more man to come and six more girls. Some people arrived this morning. Altogether there will be sixteen students, twelve girls and four men." She looked round and saw the unspoken question in the girls' eyes. "I think that I had better explain now," she continued. "There are men nurses as well as girls, although there are not so many. They make very good nurses; in fact I really do not know what we should do without them. They mainly look after the male patients, but they do go on the other wards too; they help us with the lifting of heavy patients and carrying stretchers as well as their other nursing duties."

Matron opened an inner door and called someone. A young nurse in a pink dress came into the room. "This is nurse Berita," said Matron. "She will take you over to the Nurses'

Home and show you where you are to sleep. When you have unpacked your things and had a wash, someone will take you round the Home. At half-past four you will meet sister Tutor in the sitting-room and she will have tea with you. Tomorrow morning I shall show you over the hospital. It will be very confusing at first and you will hear many words that you do not understand but, as the days go by, you will be using these words as if you had always known them and the routine of the hospital will become your life. Nurse Berita, introduce Murimi to Akolo the porter as you go out and he will take him over to the men's house."

She turned to Murimi. "You are only allowed in the Nurses' Home at certain times," she smiled, "otherwise you have your meals brought over to the men's house. You can collect the others and go over to tea at 4:30 today and you will, of course, go over to lectures; the lecture-room is just inside the front door on the right."

They followed nurse Berita out of the room.

"What's it like here?" asked Truphena.

"It is quite fun," answered Berita. "We have to work hard, but we have a day off a week and we can do what we like then. Sometimes we have dances and tournaments."

"What do you mean by tournaments?" asked a small, plump girl who had a happy-looking face.

"Well, there are lots of games we can learn to play, tennis and netball outside and table-tennis, card games and all kinds of things indoors. We are allowed to invite our friends to come, or people from the school nearby, and then we play different games and see who wins —the hospital or the visiting people!"

They went upstairs and were shown into a long room with twelve beds; there were bright patterns on the curtains, and bed covers of different colours made the room look very gay. Curtains which matched the bedspreads could be pulled round each bed, enclosing also a tall locker and a bedside table.

"If you feel you want to be on your own a bit, you can just pull those curtains," said Berita. "It's not the same as having a room to yourself, but it does give you a little place of your own. You can choose which bed you like and then I should unpack. The bathroom and toilets are just outside the door on the left. I am on duty soon, so I must go and get ready. Zipporah will be here in a few moments to show you the rest of the Home."

"I think I shall have this bed," said Rebecca, a tall, thin girl, who looked a few years older than the others. She walked over to the far corner. "It should be nice and quiet here, furthest away from the door."

Truphena chose the one opposite and the small, jolly-looking girl chose the one next to her. "What's your name?" she said to Truphena. "Mine's Mira."

"Mine's Truphena. Isn't it exciting to be here?"

"Oh yes," said Mira. "It was awful waiting for the letter to know whether or not I had been one of the lucky ones."

"What made you decide to come here?" Asked another girl, who had taken the bed the other side of Mira.

"My home is in a very lonely place," said Mira. "One day, my mother was very ill and everyone thought she would die. There was a dispensary about two hours' walk away and my father and his brothers made a stretcher by tying a blanket across two poles. Then they carried my mother to the dispensary. I was twelve then and I walked beside my mother, carrying some of her clothes. When we arrived, the man in charge said that he could not do anything for Mother and we must take her to the hospital.

Luckily, there was a landrover that was going there and we all got in; it was about twenty miles away. When we arrived, there was a great crowd and the driver told us that the people were waiting for the 'Flying Doctor'!"

"The Flying Doctor —whatever is that?" chorused the girls. By that time, everyone had gathered round Mira to hear her story. Five more students had just arrived.

"Well, I was told that doctors with special skills come from the National Hospital by plane to help the doctors at the small hospitals," Mira went on. "The people had just finished building a new place for the plane to land and they were very excited. Mother was taken into the hospital and not long afterwards the 'Flying Doctor' arrived. After a long wait, Father came to tell me that one of the nurses had said that Mother was very lucky. She needed a serious operation which only Mr. Odero could do —he was from the National Hospital. While Mother was in the hospital, Father and I stayed with some people who lived nearby. I used to go in and watch the nurses wash and feed her, make her bed and give her medicine to take the pain away. They were so kind and looked after Mother so well that I thought that I should like to be a nurse and care for sick people when I was old enough."

Then Truphena told her story and another girl, called Ruth, said that she had been at a school which was very near a hospital and had made friends with the nurses, who had interested her in their work. Ngina had once broken her arm and had been a patient for a few days and Mary had been brought to have a burn treated at the 'Out-Patients'. Lena and Traphosa had been at school together and had decided to become nurses because their school teacher had told them a little about nursing; they were both rather scared of what they

would have to do and neither of them had been near a hospital before.

"Hallo everybody! Would you like to see the rest of the Nurses' Home?" said a friendly voice from the doorway. "My name is Zipporah and I have just been given my badge of office," she said proudly, looking round to see what sort of impression she had made. No one spoke. "You see these cuffs?" She pointed to the fresh, white cuffs on her sleeves. "I am starting my second year and these show that I am not a beginner any more."

Still no one said anything. "You must feel very strange," she said in a quieter tone. "I did when I first came, but you will soon get used to everything. Come and see the games' room."

The girls followed Zipporah along the passage. Outside one of the doors she stopped and put her fingers to her lips. "Just peep in here," she said, "and don't make a noise."

She opened the door very quietly and Truphena could see about six girls fast asleep on their beds. Zipporah closed the door. "This is the room for those who are on night duty," she said. "Some people prefer to sleep in their beds, but this room is kept specially so that they will not be disturbed by the day staff. Night staff can choose which they like."

"It must be funny going to bed when everybody is getting up," said Truphena, "and it must be difficult to sleep in the daytime."

"It seems odd at first, but you soon get used to it," said Zipporah. "Sometimes, when we aren't too busy, the doctors come round and talk to us and we make tea. It is the only time that the great men take any notice of little people like us!"

The girls all laughed at this remark. Zipporah was rather large, but she was certainly full of life and very attractive. "Do any of you girls play tennis?" she asked. "We are having a tennis match next week and our best player has sprained her wrist and the new medical student Njoroge, needs a partner."

"I can play," said Rebecca. "I was Assistant Matron at a school before I came here and I used to play with the school girls sometimes."

"Oh, that's good," said Zipporah. "I'll ask Salome if she will lend you her racket."

They went downstairs and Zipporah showed them a large room with a table in the centre, which had a low net across fastened on either side. "That is for table-tennis," explained Zipporah. "If you are not too tired, come in here this evening and I'll show you how to play."

She opened some cupboards and showed shelves of different games, cards and jigsaw puzzles. One wall of the room was lined with bookshelves. "There is a note-book on the table near the books," continued Zipporah. "When you borrow a book, you must sign your name, the title of the book and the date; you can keep it for three weeks."

Down another passage was a large, bright room with many little tables; the tops were covered with blue or yellow plastic table-cloths and the curtains had a modern design of blue and black tiles. There was a large hatch at the far end and Zipporah went up to this and slid open the wooden shutters.

"What's for supper, Cook?" she called.

A lovely smell came through into the dining-room and made Truphena suddenly feel very hungry.

"There is a good supper being prepared for the new nurses," said a voice from the far side of the hatch, "but I shall not tell you what it is because there may not be enough for all the old-timers as well!"

"I know you are only teasing," said Zipporah. "Come on, girls, don't let's disturb our cooks at work! There is just time to show you the classroom and then you must go to the sitting-room to meet Sister Tutor."

Zipporah opened a door just inside the front entrance. At first, the neat rows of desks made the room seem rather like a school classroom, but when Truphena looked round, she could see glass-fronted cupboards against one wall, trolleys with gleaming utensils, bowls, basins, towels, bandages and rubber sheets.

"Look, there's someone in bed over there. Why ever is she in here?" This question came in a squeak of astonishment from Mira.

"That's Penima," said Zipporah, without a smile. "She has broken both her arms and her legs today and we have been putting them in splints and bandaging them up. Come near and say 'hallo' to her."

The girls crept after Zipporah and suddenly Rebecca said, "She is only a big doll!"

They all burst out laughing and Zipporah explained how they had to practise on 'Penima' before they were allowed to attend to the patients on the wards. Next to 'Penima' was a cot with a life-size baby and, by the side, some shelves containing baby clothes, cotton wool and talcum powder.

"We must go to the sitting-room now," said Zipporah. "You will see quite enough of this room before you have finished training."

The clock on the table showed half-past four as the girls walked into the room. Sister Njau was sitting in one of the armchairs. She had on a dark blue dress with white, frilled cuffs and a stiffly starched apron; her small white cap had a dark blue band round the front edge. Her eyes were large and she looked kindly at the girls standing nervously in the doorway. She got up and walked quickly towards a large table on the far side of the room. "Come on, nurses," she said. "Come and have some tea. Just take a plate and cup and help yourselves. Here is some bread and jam."

With quick, birdlike movements, Sister Njau poured herself out some tea, took a slice of bread and jam and went back to her armchair. "Now, pull up some chairs and let's have a talk," she said. "I hope you have recovered from your journey and don't feel too tired."

At that moment there was a loud knock on the door and in walked the four men. "Come and have some tea," said Sister. "We are just going to have a little chat."

The men came in, helped themselves to tea and sat down near Sister Njau.

"I am the Home Sister as well as Sister Tutor," she said. "So any problems you have, you must come and tell me. There are a few rules that must be kept, but we shall go over them tomorrow. The times of meals are written outside the dining-room and the bell to tell you to get up in the morning goes at seven o'clock. Our male nurses have meals brought over to their own house, but we do invite them over on special occasions," she said, her eyes twinkling. "We work hard, but we like to have some fun as well! Come to the classroom at eight o'clock tomorrow morning and you will be measured for your uniforms before Matron takes you round the hospital."

They all chatted for a few minutes. Then Sister Njau got up. "Now, I am going to leave you," she said. "Everything must seem very strange, but I hope you will all be happy here and that you will enjoy your work. Supper is at eight o'clock and I should go to bed early tonight."

She walked out of the room with quick, little steps, and everybody started talking at once.

"Be seeing you, girls," said the men, as they stood up to go.

"See you in the morning," answered Mira.

"Thanks for the tea," said Murimi.

Truphena saw Murimi looking at her with a puzzled expression. She wondered if he was trying to remember where he had seen her before.

"Let's go for a walk round the grounds," said Mira. "The flowers here are beautiful."

They stayed out for nearly an hour; then they went to their dormitory until the bell rang for supper a few minutes before eight o'clock. The food was indeed delicious; the cook had made them the "National Dish" from a recipe which had won a prize in the "All-Africa Cookery Competition" the previous year. After supper they decided to go straight to bed. Truphena thought she would stay awake for hours thinking over the events of the day, but she hardly had time to say good night to Mira before she fell into a deep, dreamless sleep.

Chapter 2

On Tour with Matron

The next morning Truphena was awakened by the sound of a loud bell. She opened her eyes and looked around. At first she could not think where she was; then she saw Mira jump out of bed and suddenly the long room was full of chattering girls. "Come on, Sleepy," said Mira, "race you to the bathroom!"

Truphena pushed back the blankets, stretched, and with a bound she was at the door before Mira. Laughing, the two girls made for the bathrooms and before long they had returned, dressed and were running along the passage to the dining room.

Truphena ate a large breakfast and so did most of her companions, all except Lena and Traphosa, who felt very strange and shy. After a second cup of tea, Truphena went up to tidy her bed and was soon joined by the others. Then they all went downstairs to the classroom.

Sister Njau was there with the tailor from the village, and without delay the girls were measured for their uniforms. "They will all be ready by the end of the week," said the tailor. "I'll bring them along myself and make sure they fit."

Footsteps were heard along the passage and in a few moments, Matron appeared. The girls stood up. "Good morning! I hope you have slept well and had a good breakfast," said Matron, "because we have a busy morning ahead."

At that moment, there was a knock on the door; without waiting for an answer, in walked the four men students, looking very smart in their new white coats.

When they saw Matron, they stopped. "I am sorry we are late," said Murimi, "but all our watches said different times."

"You must set your watches by the hospital clock," said Matron, rather crossly. "You must always make a habit of being punctual, then you will never be late on duty. Nurses cannot leave the wards until someone has come to take over from them; so, if you are late, it means that you are making someone else work overtime."

She turned to the others. "As we go round the hospital, I shall tell you about the wards. This hospital has a hundred and fifty-five beds altogether and the patients are put in different wards, depending on what is wrong with them." She wrote the names of the wards on the blackboard.

"There are two places where we shall not go today," she continued. "The Maternity Ward is where mothers come to have their babies. Newborn babies can catch diseases very easily, so it is better that no one should go near them except their mothers and those who are working on that ward. The other place where we shall not go is the Infectious Diseases Ward, where people are nursed who have illness such as measles, chicken-pox, poliomyelitis and whooping-cough, that are easily passed on to others. That reminds me, you must all go over to the 'Out-Patients' and have your inoculations at four o'clock this afternoon."

The students looked rather alarmed. "Don't worry," said Matron. "They are to prevent you from catching certain diseases like typhoid, tetanus and so on. How many of you had inoculations when you were children?" she asked.

About half the class put up their hands. Truphena remembered again about Benaiah —"I shall never forget that he nearly died," she said, half aloud.

"What was that?" said Matron.

Truphena looked confused. "I was thinking of my young brother and what happened when he had tetanus," she said quietly.

Matron knew why Truphena had chosen to be a nurse and she nodded sympathetically.

"If you have all the inoculations that we advise, then you can help to educate other people, especially mothers, to bring their children here. Your job as a nurse is not only to care for the sick, but to try to prevent illness as well."

Matron walked towards the door. "Let's go now."

They walked across the lawn to the main hospital building and went inside. Truphena wrinkled up her nose. "That is called a 'hospital smell'," said Matron, watching her. "It is the disinfectant that kills the germs. Germs are our enemy; they love dirt, so it is our job to get rid of dirt and dust. Everything, including the floors, is washed with some kind of disinfectant each day."

Matron pushed open a swing door and immediately a nurse in a pink dress ran to hold it open for her. "This is the Women's Medical Ward," explained Matron. "Patients in here need medicine and rest: often their treatment takes quite a long time and sometimes several different medicines have to be tried before a patient fully recovers. There are twenty-two beds in here and twenty-two on the men's side."

The students saw a long room with beds on either side. Most of the beds were occupied, but two patients were sitting on chairs and another was walking slowly down the passage in between the rows of beds. A nurse in a light blue dress with a blue band round her cap came up to Matron and said good morning. "Good morning, Staff," said Matron. "I am bringing my new nurses round the hospital."

She turned to the students, who were standing behind her. "Ward Sister has a day off today and Staff Nurse is in charge. She has two Assistant Nurses under her, also two third-year students and two second-year. In a few weeks' time you will start working on the wards. You will spend three months on each ward. You can help the senior nurses a great deal, even whilst you are learning, but, of course, you will not be expected to take on too much responsibility."

Matron went towards an old lady who was sitting up in bed in the corner. "How is your pain today, Mrs. Nomeka?" she asked.

"It was very bad this morning," replied the patient, "but one of the nice young nurses gave me a warm rubber bottle to hold over it and now it is much better."

Matron went over to talk to a girl who was about Truphena's age and was looking very sad. "What is the matter, Elima?" she asked. "You will be going home in a few days' time."

Elima turned over on her face and did not speak.

"Tell me," said Matron, "is there anything we can do to help you?"

"I have been here so long that I have missed the chance to take school certificate and I don't think my father can pay my fees any longer," answered Elima, in a stifled voice.

"Which school do you go to?" asked Matron. Elima told her.

"The headmistress there is a friend of mine; I shall write and ask her if anything can be done. But please cheer up. You have been so ill that it is wonderful that you can even think of studying again so soon."

Elima turned over and sat up with a brave smile.

In a corner of the ward, Truphena noticed a nurse holding a mask over a patient's face. "Whatever is she doing?" she asked, in a loud voice.

"Hush," said Matron, "that patient came in just a short time ago. She has pneumonia and cannot breathe very well. The mask is attached to the cylinder you can see by the side of the bed; that contains a gas called oxygen, and nurse is holding the mask so that the patient can breathe more easily. Now, let's go and see how the men are this morning, but first I shall show you the 'sluice'!"

She opened a door and the students peeped into a small room with two deep sinks, bowls, bed-pans, rubber sheets and drying racks.

"This is where all the utensils used on the ward are washed, and any stained or soiled sheets are rinsed before they are sent down to the laundry. There is a room like this attached to every ward."

She walked through the swing door opposite the sluice. "I want a shave, Nurse," said a loud voice. "Sh-h-h!" said a little nurse in pink, standing near one of the patients.

"What is the matter, Chinua?" laughed Matron, "Aren't my nurses looking after you properly?"

Some of the students giggled and the man in the bed next to Chinua said, "You had better be careful what you say or Matron will make you grow a beard and then your wife won't know you when you go home!"

At that there was a loud burst of laughter.

"Don't make so much noise," said Matron. "You will disturb Mr. Odolo."

She walked over to one of the beds and looked down at a very old, man, who lay still, with his eyes closed.

"This old man came in a week ago," she explained.

"He collapsed whilst he was working on his land. His son brought him to the hospital and Doctor says he must stay, and rest as he has something wrong with his heart. He sleeps most of the time."

They walked along a passage to the next ward. "This is the Women's Surgical Ward," said Matron. "It is always a very busy place. Patients here are being prepared for operations or else they have had an operation and are recovering. We try to keep as quiet as possible, but it is a noisier place than the Medical Ward."

Matron spoke to some of the patients and comforted a young girl who had been in a car accident and was going to have an operation on her foot. One bed had screens round and a nurse was pushing a trolley towards it.

"That patient has had a stomach operation and nurse is going to put a clean dressing on the wound," said Matron. "The old lady in the corner, who is sleeping, has been given an injection to make her drowsy before she goes for her operation later this morning."

They looked into the 'duty room' and saw gleaming instruments and a large steel tank from which steam was pouring. "That is a 'sterilizer'," said Matron. "It is not enough just to wash the things we use, but they must be boiled as well, to make sure that all the germs are killed, so that nothing will stop the operation wounds from healing quickly."

They walked through the Men's Surgical Ward and across a covered way to the Children's Ward. As Matron opened the door, there was a burst of happy laughter. "Nursie," sang one little child. "Play with me, Nurse." "Nurse, I want a drink." All the voices seemed to be shouting at once. The ward contained thirty-five cots, with sides that could be pulled up so that the children could not get out.

"I thought the children would be unhappy here," said Truphena.

"When they first come in, they are often frightened and cry for their mothers, but they soon settle down and grow very fond of the nurses. When a child is very sick, we encourage the mother to stay and screen off a corner of the ward for them."

One little boy was lying on his back, with his legs bandaged and strung up to a wooden bar fixed above the bed. He was gurgling happily.

"What has happened to him?" asked Rebecca. She loved children and wanted to be a children's nurse when she had finished her training.

"That little chap had something wrong with the bones on his hips," explained Matron. "He had his operation two weeks ago and now he is quite used to that position and doesn't seem to mind it at all."

As they went out, two nurses were taking round mugs of milk. The students agreed that they would all look forward to their work on that ward.

"Now we shall go to the 'Theatre'," said Matron. Some of the students looked puzzled. "That is where the doctors perform all the operations," she continued. "The theatre nurses are cleaning up at the moment as doctor will not be operating until later in the morning."

They went into a small room where there were bottles, basins, sinks and cylinders, trolleys with scissors, forceps, basins, rubber gloves and bandages. Matron opened a cupboard and showed the neat rows of long, green gowns and shelves with caps, masks, sheets and blankets. The smell of disinfectant was stronger there than anywhere else in the hospital.

Truphena noticed a huge tank, like the one in the sluice

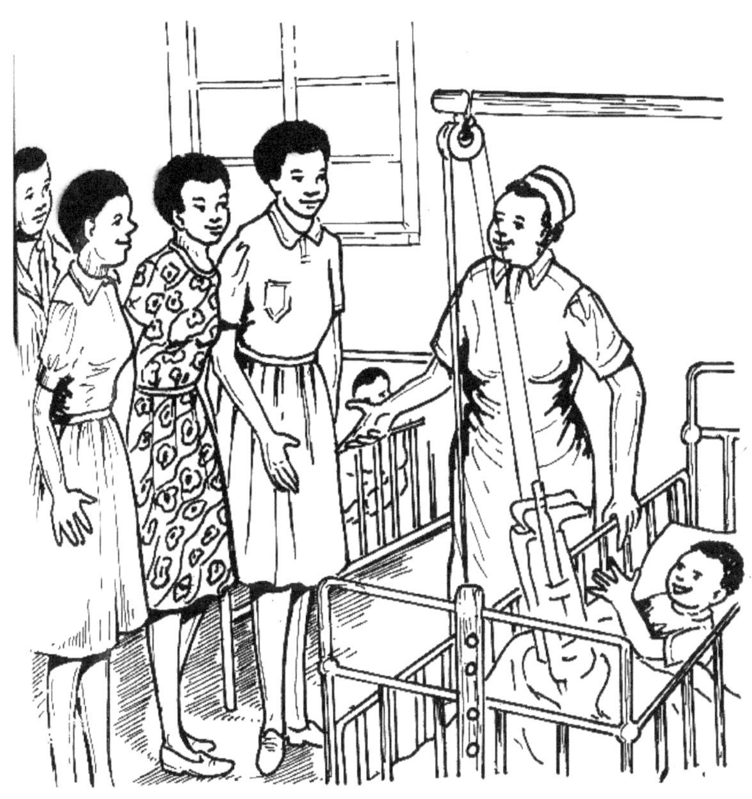

He had his operation two weeks ago and now he is quite used to that position ..."

of the Surgical Ward and she saw one of the nurses open the lid and put in a bowl, with a long pair of forceps. "Look at the enormous sterilizer!" she said.

Matron nodded with approval. "Yes," she said. "Of course everything in here must be scrupulously clean. Most things can be boiled, but gowns, bandages and towels are sterilized by steam, under pressure, in this apparatus —it is called an 'autoclave'." She pointed to something that looked rather like an oven.

She went across to a row of cylinders, rather larger than the ones Truphena had noticed in the Medical Ward. "These cylinders contain anaesthetic," she went on. "A mask attached to the cylinders is held over the patient's face. The patient breathes in gas from the cylinders and goes to sleep. She knows nothing until she finds herself back in bed in the ward."

She took a pile of cloth masks from one of the shelves in the cupboard.

"Try these on," she said, and handed them round. She called Truphena and showed how to tie the mask so that it covered her nose and mouth.

"It feels funny," said Truphena, in a muffled voice. "I could not keep this on for long."

"You soon get used to it," said Matron. "You wear them whenever you go into the operating theatre and also when you look after newborn babies if ever you have a cold when you are on duty; then you don't breathe germs over the patient or anything you use."

The students followed Matron into the theatre. They noticed the white painted wall and, in the centre of the room, a flat table, above this was a huge, round light, larger than a bicycle wheel. Matron switched on the light and moved it round. "This is made so that it can shine exactly onto the part of the patient where the doctor is going to operate."

She waited a few moments so they could take a careful look round the theatre. "There is just time to see the X-ray Department. It is near the 'Out-Patients', but we must hurry now."

They walked along another corridor and into a room darkened by black curtains. When they had become used to the gloom, they saw a large apparatus, with a big hood, beside a table rather like the operating table.

"That is the X-ray machine," said Matron. "The patient lies on the table and the films go underneath the part where the doctor wants a picture taken."

"She opened a drawer and pulled out a large, black piece of paper, and drawing back one of the curtains, held it up to the light. The students could plainly see two long bones and, across one of them, a thin line.

"Do you remember one of the children in the ward with her arm bandaged?" she asked. "This is a picture of the bones in her arm and the line across one of the bones shows where it has been broken; when the doctor saw this, he knew exactly how to set the bone."

"What a good idea," gasped Lena in surprise, her interest quite overcoming her shyness. "That's a wonderful thing; I never knew anything like that existed before."

"Some of you may have been here for treatment," said Matron, as they walked passed the 'Out-Patients'. "That is Dr. Loice Onyango on duty; she is a great favourite with the children."

"Do girls become doctors?" asked Traphosa. It was the first time she had spoken.

"Yes," answered Matron. "We have both male nurses and lady doctors here! I know that seems strange to some of you. Now it is your lunch-time. Next time I see you, I hope you will have your uniforms. Good-bye."

"Good-bye, Matron, and thank you," they chorused.

As Truphena, deep in thought, was walking towards the Nurses' Home, Murimi came striding up to her. "You were the brave little girl I met carrying your brother to hospital, weren't you?" he asked.

"Yes, that's right," answered Truphena. "I recognized you on the bus."

"I'm glad he recovered," said Murimi.

"Yes," said Truphena, "that is why I decided to come here."

Chapter 3

Work and Play

The men were already in the classroom when Truphena, Mira and the others arrived. Punctually at 2.30, Sister Njau walked in. "Did you enjoy your tour of the hospital this morning?" she asked.

Everyone said that they did.

"I am going to give you each some note-books, a pen, pencil and a pair of scissors," she said. "Wherever you go, always carry the small notebook, the pen, pencil and scissors with you; you never know when you might need them."

When everything had been handed out, Sister walked over to a cupboard.

"Now, I shall introduce you to Johnson," she said. She opened the door, and there, dangling from a large hook, was a life-size skeleton! Everyone gasped.

"This is Johnson," said Sister, in her quick, little voice. "He lets us examine him and learn where all his bones are and how one fits into another."

"Was he ever real?" asked Truphena, in a whisper.

"Certainly he was," answered Sister. "He was a patient who had been ill for a very long time. Before he died, he said he would like his bones to be used for teaching purposes because he was so grateful for all the care he had been given while he was in hospital."

"Can you take anybody's bones like that?" asked Lena, with a shudder.

"No, indeed you can't," answered Sister. "A person must say before he dies that he wants his bones used in this way."

She opened the door, and there, dangling from a large hook, was a life-size skeleton!

"I think it was very kind of Johnson, whoever he was," said Rebecca. "Perhaps I shall do the same."

"Come and have a closer look at him," said Sister. They all went to the skeleton and sister let them gently move his arms and legs.

"How many bones are there altogether?" asked Truphena.

"There are over two hundred," answered Sister, "and each one has a special job to do. You will learn about them all in time."

She closed the cupboard door and went over to the bed and cot. "Come and see our patients," she said. "This is Penima and this is baby Indire."

The girls had already seen these the day before, so it was the men's turn to look surprised.

"We bath these models, dress and undress them, bandage them and pretend they have many different kinds of illness. After a while, you become quite fond of them and almost think of them as real people!"

Sister Njau then pointed to the picture hanging above her desk. It showed an old lady in a long dress; she had a shawl round her shoulders and a little round cap on her head. Truphena noticed the intelligent expression on her face, full of strength, pity and kindness.

"I expect you should like to know who this lady is," said Sister. "Sit down and I shall tell you about her."

The students went back to their desks and looked at Sister expectantly.

"The lady in the picture is called Florence Nightingale," she began. "Her parents had plenty of money and did not want her to do any work. However, she made up her mind that she would help the sick. At that time, hospitals were dirty places, not at all like they are today, and there were no trained nurses. Miss Nightingale studied in France and Germany and then took charge of a small hospital in London. At that time the British and Russians were at war and she was asked to go where they were fighting to look after wounded soldiers. She had to nurse them in very bad conditions, and several times became very ill herself. When the war was over, people were so grateful to her that they gave a large sum of money and she used it to start the first real school of nursing at St. Thomas' Hospital, London. That was over a hundred years ago. Even today, nurses who train at St. Thomas' are called 'Nightingales'."

Everyone started to ask questions about this wonderful person, and Sister gave them the names of some books to read which, she said, were in the games' room library. She told the men that they could use the library at certain times each day.

"Tomorrow, we shall start classes on the Principles of Nursing," continued Sister. "You will not be going on the wards yet, except to be shown things that you have learnt in class."

A sigh of disappointment went round the room.

"Yes, I know you want to start looking after the patients straight away," said Sister, sympathetically, "but it just cannot be done. You need to practise on Penima and Indire —and on each other —before you can be allowed to look after sick people."

"When we do go on the wards, are we supposed to talk to the patients?" asked Truphena.

"Well, you can't spend too much time talking, but often a little chat will be a great comfort to someone who has to lie in bed all day. Remember that many people have never been inside a hospital before and they are frightened to be away from their own surroundings and amongst strange people. They often don't understand what is happening to them or why. Some people have been treated by witch doctors but have not been cured and, because they still partly believe in magic, they are scared of modern treatment. You must be extra sympathetic with them. Remember that at one time everyone believed that illness was caused by evil spirits. A Greek physician, called Hippocrates, was the first person to realize that illness was caused by something not working properly inside your body. He watched sick people carefully and wrote down the signs of their illness; he also wrote down notes on how patients should be examined and cared for and doctors still follow his teaching. He lived over two thousand five hundred years ago and is called the father of medicine."

"In Africa, the old and the new work side by side," remarked Murimi. "That must make our work rather difficult."

"That is true," replied Sister, "and since you are going to be a dispenser and work in a remote part of the country, you will come across many examples of this. You will have to explain to people why they should come to you first when they are ill. When everybody understands how modern medicine can help them, witch doctors will die out because no one will go to them. Education and prevention of disease are just as important parts of our work as actually nursing the sick."

"How can we prevent disease?" asked Onyango, a quiet man, who was sitting next to Murimi.

"There are several ways," replied Sister. "One is to encourage people to eat the right kinds of food; another is to persuade them to bring their children to hospitals or dispensaries for inoculations against certain types of illness. Teaching cleanliness in the home is another way and also keeping sick people away from others so that their illness does not spread.”

Sister looked at her watch. “Goodness me, it is time for you to go for your inoculations now and then your tea will be ready. I shall expect you here at half-past eight sharp tomorrow morning.”

As they went out of the room, Murimi waited for Truphena. “Will you come for a walk after tea?” he asked. Truphena had promised to go with Mira, but she was longing to talk to Murimi. For a moment she did not know what to say.

“Why don’t you bring a friend and I’ll ask Onyango to come too?” suggested Murimi, appearing to read her thoughts. Truphena turned to Mira, who was standing behind her.

“Would you like to go?” she asked.

“Oh yes, that would be great fun,” said Mira. “We’ll meet you outside the Nurses’ Home in twenty minutes.”

The girls were excited and after a hurried tea they ran out of the Nurses’ Home and found Murimi and Onyango waiting for them.

“Where would you like to go?” asked Murimi.

“Let’s go and see if anyone is playing tennis,” suggested Truphena.

They set off round the side of the Nurses’ Home and soon they could hear the ‘ping’ of a ball against a racket.

“There are Rebecca and Zipporah,” said Mira, “and those must be two of the medical students. By the way, why aren’t you and Murimi studying with them?”

“We are not training to be doctors,” said Onyango. “We are going to be nurses, like you.”

“But Sister said something about Murimi going to be a dispenser; that needs a doctor’s training, doesn’t it?” she asked.

"No," answered Onyango, "but many people do think that dispensers are doctors which they are not, although they certainly have a very responsible job. Often they are in charge of the only medical facilities for miles around."

"Can girls be dispensers too?" asked Truphena.

"I don't know of any," answered Murimi. "It would be rather a lonely life for them, but I suppose there is no reason why they can't. The best thing would be for a dispenser to marry a nurse and then they could both work together. Neither of them would be lonely then!"

Murimi looked down at Truphena. She was slim and pretty and he found her very attractive. There was a moment's silence.

"Hallo, you four," shouted Zipporah. "Come and meet Njoroge and Festus."

"Don't stop your game for us; we'll just watch," said Murimi.

"We were only practising; it wasn't a real game," said Njoroge. "Do any of you play?"

"No, but we should like to try," answered Murimi, "only we haven't any rackets."

"Or shoes," added Onyango.

"Why don't you try on our shoes and see if they fit well enough for now?" suggested Zipporah.

The eight of them sat on the grass at the edge of the court and tried on each other's shoes, amidst much laughter. "Why, Rebecca, yours fit Onyango. You must have large feet!" said Zipporah.

"My feet are fat, let me try Njoroge's," said Mira.

"Don't you call my feet fat," said Njoroge, in a voice that sounded as if she had insulted him.

"I didn't. I said that my feet were fat," said poor Mira, very embarrassed.

Suddenly, they found that all the shoes had been thrown in a pile. They all laughed heartily while they sorted them out; eventually, the four newcomers were fitted out.

"We'll go on one side and the girls can go on the other," said Murimi.

"Oh no! That's not fair," said Truphena. "You will be sure to beat us."

"No, we won't beat you. It's old-fashioned to beat women these days!" said Murimi, with a huge grin.

"Come on, let's start," said Mira. "Where is the ball?"

"Here, catch!" Rebecca threw her a ball. "Now, hit it over the net. It must bounce once on the other side and then Murimi or Onyango must try to hit it back. It must not go outside the white lines or it is a point to the other side."

For the next half hour, there was a lot of laughter as Truphena and Mira, Murimi and Onyango ran about after the ball. Murimi once hit it so hard that it went into the garden of the Nurses' Home. Zipporah said that if Sister Tutor saw she would say that Murimi had done it on purpose. Murimi said that he had not, but it was an idea for the future! They became so hot and tired and they felt they had had enough.

"Let's watch you now and see how the game should really be played," puffed Murimi.

They all changed shoes once more and the first four went on to the court. Festus asked Rebecca to be his partner and Zipporah went on the other side with Njoroge.

It was a good game; Rebecca played well. She was a tall, graceful girl and never seemed to be excited or run about much, but she was always in the right place to hit the ball.

"She will make a good nurse," said a quiet voice.

Truphena looked up and saw Matron standing beside her, watching the game with keen interest.

Nursing did not seem to have much to do with tennis, but seeing Rebecca's calm face and controlled movements, Truphena thought she understood what patron meant.

Chapter 4

On the Wards

It was just a month after the students had arrived when Lena and Traphosa disappeared. Everyone was sitting in the classroom; there was a feeling of excitement in the air because, the day before, they had been told that they would all spend the morning on the wards. This, at last, was the work they had come to do —to be amongst patients, nurses and doctors.

It was Sister Njau who first noticed that there were two empty desks in the room. "Where are Lena and Traphosa?" she asked.

Everyone looked round. Truphena remembered that she had not seen them at breakfast, but she had been rather late as she could not fix her cap properly, so she thought they had probably had their breakfast earlier. She offered to go up to the dormitory to see if, perhaps, they were not feeling well. When she returned, she had a troubled look on her face. "They've gone," she said in a hushed voice. "Their uniforms are on their beds and their cupboards and drawers are empty."

Everyone looked shocked. Suddenly they were all talking at one.

"They must have run away!"

"Perhaps they were scared because they had to go on the wards."

"They did find the lectures rather difficult and Lena cried when Doctor asked her a question and she couldn't answer."

"I did hear Traphosa say that she didn't know she would have to work so hard!"

"Stop all this noise," said Sister. "I must tell Matron at once. You can be looking at your notes while I go over to the hospital; I shall be giving you a test next week. I shall be back in twenty minutes; try to keep quiet while I am gone."

"I wish we had made more effort to know them better," whispered Truphena to Mira. "Perhaps if we had been more friendly, they wouldn't have run away."

"They only seemed to want to talk to each other," answered Mira. "I did ask Lena once if she would like to come and watch the tennis, but she said she was going to the shops with Traphosa; when I said I'd go with them, they just giggled and said it was all right."

"Do they live far away from here, do you know?" asked Truphena.

"I think it is about forty miles," replied Mira, "but of course we had our pocket money yesterday, so they could afford the fare. There is a bus that passes here every morning about eight o'clock, but I don't know how near to their homes it would take them."

They tried to settle down to work, but with all the excitement, they managed to do no more than read the same page over and over again. It seemed much longer than twenty minutes before Sister returned.

"Matron has asked me to tell you not to talk about the two girls disappearing to anyone over at the hospital. It is very disturbing when anything like this happens. They must have gone off when you were all having breakfast; it is a busy time then and no one would have noticed them go. Matron will have to drive to their homes later today to see if they are there. Try to forget about this upset for the moment and we will go to the wards. I told you yesterday where you were to work, so put away your books and follow me."

Truphena and Mira were to work on the Surgical Ward. "Now, remember, do everything Sister or Staff Nurse tells you —and do it well!" said Sister Njau, with a smile, as she left them.

They went through the door and into the ward, feeling very self-conscious in their new pink dresses and starched caps and aprons.

They went up to Sister, who was writing something at a little table just inside the ward. "Excuse us...," began Truphena.

Sister looked up. "Oh, you are the new students, are you? Well, we are very busy in here, so you must not get in anyone's way. Doctor hasn't done his round yet, so just see that all the beds look neat and tidy; then you can go to the sluice and wash out some mackintoshes. You'll find nurse Berita in there."

Mira and Truphena walked down the two rows of beds, straightening a sheet here, a pillow there and seeing that the patients were comfortable.

In the sluice they found Berita leaning over a large sink, washing a rubber sheet. They watched her rinse it, dry it and hang it over a wooden rail.

"Have you two come to help me with this pile?" she asked, pointing to a mound of rubbers beside her.

Mira and Truphena were glad to see Berita again; they had hardly spoken to her since the day they arrived and she had taken them to the Nurses' Home.

"Yes, Sister told us to come in here," said Truphena. "What a lot to wash," she remarked.

"Yes, there is always a lot on this ward," said Berita, "but I don't think that there is as much as on the Children's Ward. We're always washing out sheets in here."

"You don't wash dirty bedclothes, do you?" asked Truphena.

"Well, we have to rub the stains out before they go to the hospital laundry, and we soak them in disinfectant if they are very soiled," answered Berita.

"I didn't realize that nurses had to do those sort of things," said Mira.

"No, many people don't, but who would do them if we didn't?" replied Berita.

"I suppose it is just the way you think about it," said Truphena, wisely. "If you think of yourself or one of your family lying in bed sick, then you don't mind so much what you do."

They chatted on and soon the last mackintosh was washed, dried and laid over the wooden rollers. "Now let's wash the rubber rings. There are only four to do," said Berita.

"What are those for?" asked Truphena.

"After certain operations, it is more comfortable for the patients if they are supported by these instead of lying flat on the bed. Beds can feel very hard if you have to lie in one position for a long time," explained Berita. "Actually, we don't let anyone lie too long in one position in case they get bed-sores; if a patient cannot move herself, we turn her over every few hours."

"There is such a lot to remember to do," said Truphena. "I am sure I shall forget something."

"No, you won't," said Berita. "Everything is done at certain times, so it is not likely you will forget —anyway, if you do, Sister or Staff Nurse will remind you pretty quickly!"

"Sister looked a bit cross when I came in," said Truphena. "Is is difficult to work under her?"

"Sister Naome is a wonderful person," said Berita enthusiastically. "At first lots of people think she is rather sharp, but when a patient is ill or frightened, she has endless patience. Mind you, she has no sympathy for people who make a fuss over nothing and she is certainly annoyed if a nurse does something stupid. But don't be frightened of her; she is quick to notice people who will make good nurses and she gives people responsible jobs as soon as she thinks they can do them, so work here is very interesting."

Male voices were heard outside. "There is Doctor coming now," said Berita, opening the door a crack. Truphena and Mira peeped out. Sister was leading the way, looking very important in her dark blue uniform. She went up to the first bed and handed the doctor a folder containing the notes on the patient's treatment and progress.

"That's Doctor Njoroge, the House Surgeon," said Berita. "He does most of the operating and has been here for a number of years. Last week, Sister let me go in the operating theatre and watch him. The two medical students were there and he explained everything to them as he went along. He made it so clear, that even I could understand most of it! At first, it seemed as if he wasn't treating the patient as a person at all, but when he had finished, he turned to Sister Naome and said, 'Take good care of this lady, Sister. Remember her family is relying on us to make her well again. It is not the same at home without mother!' So I realized that he was thinking about her after all."

At that moment, a little nurse rushed in with an armful of sheets. "Quick, could you rinse out these for me?" she asked breathlessly. "Old man Hudson has just disgraced himself again—and just as the Doctor is coming round too! I've changed everything and I must go back to see that he is quite comfortable."

She dashed out, leaving a pile of sheets. Berita sighed. "Oh, well," she said, "I suppose it's part of our job, and Hudson is such a dear old man! He was knocked down by a car about a fortnight ago and cannot move his legs. He has had one operation, but he has to have at least two more and even then we shall not know for a long time whether or not he will walk again. He is one of the oldest men in the village and he used to collect all the children round him and tell them stories of the time when he was a boy. In spite of his injury, he is always cheerful and he teases Matron when she comes round. He is the only one who dares to do that!"

"Is he in much pain?" asked Truphena.

"No, that is the tragedy, in a way," answered Berita. "He cannot feel anything; if he could, we would know he was getting better. When I first washed him, I was afraid of hurting him. Sister told me he couldn't feel anything but, she said, because of that I must be extra gentle and dry his legs well so that they would not get sore."

"What, three of you in here! And you all look as if you have nothing to do and all day to do it in! Come along and take the bed-pans round." It was Sister Naome.

The bed-pans were in the sluice, on a rack opposite the sink. Beside the rack was a wash-place; tins of disinfectant stood nearby. Truphena remembered how each pan had to be rinsed with hot water and then wiped round with disinfecant. It was not a pleasant job but, once again, she tried to imagine herself ill in bed and unable to get up. She thought how glad she would be that there were nurses to care for her. Mira thought of the time when her mother was ill and how cheerfully the nurses had looked after her then.

"Will you help me lift mother Fenora?" asked Berita. "She has had an operation on one of her lungs and has to stay in a sitting position. She has slipped down a little and has to be careful how she moves."

Truphena followed Berita towards the bed at the end of the ward.

"Hallo, my daughters," said the old lady. "Have you come to help an old woman? Ah, here is a new nurse. How do you like looking after an old nuisance like me, my dear?"

"You aren't a nuisance and I love looking after you!" The words came out before Truphena realized what she was saying.

As the old lady thanked her, she felt tears pricking the back of her eyes. She thought what a wonderful thing it was to be able to help the sick. Pity and understanding were growing within her. She looked up and saw that Berita had pulled the curtain round the bed.

"Always pull the curtains or put up screens when attending to a patient," she said.

"Oh dear," sighed Truphena, and repeated for the hundredth time that she would never remember everything she had to do.

"Whenever possible, think that it is yourself lying in bed and then you will find you will often remember things which otherwise you might forget. Nursing is hard work; if we didn't like it, we couldn't stay."

For the first time since she had arrived on the ward, Truphena thought about Lena and Traphosa. "If we didn't like it, we couldn't stay," Berita had just said. "Perhaps she is right," thought Truphena. But at that moment, she found it difficult to think that anyone could possibly not like nursing.

Half an hour later, Sister Naome came up to Truphena. "Now, you go in the men's ward and clean their lockers, Nurse. You can clean those in here," she said to Mira, who had come to see what she should do next. "I am glad you two were sent here today; we have been extra busy and I don't know how we should have managed to clean everything properly if it hadn't been for you. You understand that in the Surgical Ward it is especially important to have everything free from germs."

Truphena went shyly into the men's ward. "Here's a new nurse," said a young man in the bed nearest the door. "Have you come to cheer us up?"

"Now, Samweli, let Nurse do her work." This remark came from a girl in a pink dress with a narrow black band round her cap. Truphena knew from the cap that she was a third-year student. She wondered if she would ever reach that stage; it seemed a long way ahead just now.

As she went up to the locker beside the first bed, Truphena realized that she had not collected anything to clean it with. Back she went to the sluice and looked round for something she could use as a 'damp duster' and cloth. She remembered that 'dry-dusting' just spread the germs. Berita looked in at that moment. "Where are the dusting things?" asked Truphena.

Berita opened a drawer and gave her some cloths.

"Don't forget to wash them out when you have finished," she said. "Here, take this bowl!" She handed a bowl of water to Truphena, who walked slowly back to the ward.

Truphena carefully put down the bowl of water on top of the first locker and started to clear off the things. I see that we have an extra pair of hands today," said a voice in the doorway.

Truphena swung round and as she did so, she knocked the bowl onto the floor. A river of water seemed to flow towards Matron's feet. Truphena stood there Helplessly as the third-year nurse rushed for a floor cloth.

"These things will happen," said Matron in a calm voice.

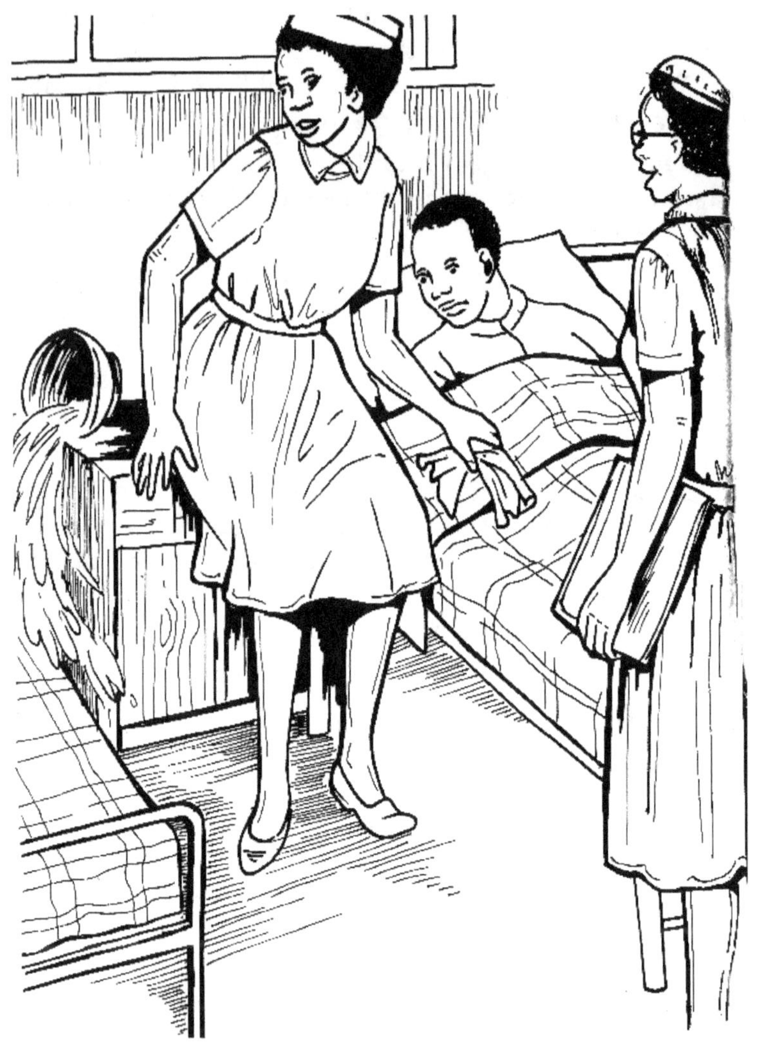

Hearing her, Truphena felt normal again.

"I-I-I'm sorry. Matron," she stammered. "I knocked the bowl over."

"Yes, I can see that," said Matron, "and I suppose you are thinking what a lot of water can come out of a little bowl!"

As that was exactly what Truphena was thinking she could not help smiling.

"I hear you have been working very hard this morning," said Matron, "but a good nurse must keep calm and not become over-excited. Think of what you are doing all the time and let nothing surprise you!"

Matron walked down the ward, saying a few words to every patient. By the time she had left, Truphena had recovered from her embarrassment and was carefully washing and drying the lockers, just as she had learnt in the classroom 'ward'. As she finished putting back the patient's belongings on the last locker, Sister called her to help hand round the lunches. A huge trolley had been brought along from the kitchens and two nurses were needed to push it down the centre of the ward. Staff Nurse came to attend to two patients on special diets, and Truphena and Berita handed round trays to the others.

"It is your lunch-time now, so you had better go," Sister told them when they had finished. "Sister Njau will say that I overwork her students and then they are too tired to listen to her lectures in the afternoon. You have worked well; I shall look forward to having you on my ward again."

"That was praise indeed!" whispered Berita, who had heard Sister Naome's remarks. "That means a good report to Matron for you."

Chapter 5

The Accident

Next morning, as Sister Tutor was about to begin a lecture, Matron walked into the room, looking very grave.

"Excuse me, Sister," she said. "I want to talk to everybody for a few minutes." She turned to the students. "You must all be wanting to know what has happened to Lena and Traphosa."

A murmur went round the class.

"As I was driving to their homes yesterday afternoon, I was stopped on the way by two women. They said there had been an accident and asked me to go to their house. It appears that the girls had stopped a taxi going in the direction of their home and, after travelling only a few miles, there had been an accident. The taxi had gone round the corner rather fast and had swerved across the wrong side of the road; it had crashed into a car coming in the opposite direction. Both drivers had been killed and some of the passengers badly injured. Very scared, but apparently unhurt, Lena and Traphosa had run off and found shelter in the home of one of the villagers, who turned out to be Lena's cousin.

"Lena had escaped with a few bruises. Traphosa seemed perfectly all right at first, but later in the day she became unconscious. Lena's cousin had become very worried and had gone to the road to find someone who would help her. It was then, luckily, that I came along."

She paused for a moment. The students waited silently for her to finish her story.

"I went to the house and asked Lena's cousin to help me carry Traphosa back to my car. When Lena saw me, she burst into tears and asked if she could come with me and help nurse

Traphosa. She had been resting in my house since I brought her back, but this morning I am going to let her go over to the ward and work there until Traphosa is fit to leave. You will be pleased to hear that the doctor says Traphosa will be completely cured in time, but she will need very careful nursing.”

Matron turned to Sister Tutor. “Sister, Lena and Traphosa have had enough punishment for running away,” she said. “I understand from Lena that they did not want to do what they called the ‘dirty jobs’ around the ward. Now that tragedy has touched their lives, they will think differently, I am sure. I am not going to persuade either of them to carry on with their training if they don’t want to do so but, if they decided to stay, I think they will be an example to future students. Will you agree that Lena may be excused from lectures until Traphosa is well enough to leave the hospital? That should be in about two months’ time.”

“It is a miracle that they are both alive,” said Sister Njau. “I think that it is an excellent idea for Lena to help to nurse Traphosa. By the end of that time she will certainly be able to decide whether or not she wants to continue her studies. Thank you for telling us everything. Matron. I am sure the students will do all they can to make Lena’s life pleasant when she is off duty.”

As Matron walked out, she smiled kindly at the students. “Work hard,” she said. “You will be spending more time on the wards from now on, but you must not neglect your studies. Everything you learn in the classroom will help you to understand what you are doing on the wards; understanding why you do things will make you better nurses.”

“Matron is very sensible,” said Truphena to Mira. “It is easier to do your work when you understand the reason for it.”

"Yes," answered Mira, "and she is very human, too. I should never have thought of letting Lena go on the wards after running away like that, but I can see what a good idea it is. Lena will probably make a better nurse than any of us now!"

The rest of the morning flew by. First, Sister passed round different bones and the students had to draw them, name them and write a few notes on their use in the body. Then, one by one, they went up to Johnson, the skeleton, and found a similar bone to the one they had been given; they showed the class where it was and how it would be used. After that, the students took partners and practised bed-making and laying up trolleys for different operations and dressings. In no time at all the bell rang for lunch.

As Truphena and Mira were going into the dining- room, they saw Lena coming along the passage. "Let's ask her to sit with us," said Truphena.

She went up to Lena and asked her how she was.

"I hear you are a real nurse now," she said. "How is Traphosa?"

"She opened her eyes and looked at me about half an hour ago, but I don't think she recognized me," answered Lena sadly. "Oh, I do hope she gets better. It was my fault that she ran away. I think she would have stayed if I had not kept asking her to come with me. She thought she would get used to the work, but I persuaded her that nursing wasn't the job for us."

"What were you going to do then?" asked Truphena.

"We thought we would go to the town and find some sort of work; we hadn't really decided what to do exactly. It was exciting creeping out of the Nurses' Home when you were all having breakfast. We thought someone would see us, so when we saw the taxi coming along, we stopped it. Then there was the accident. We were terribly scared and when we realized we were all right, we got out and ran away. It was not until afterwards that I felt bad about leaving the injured passengers.

"We went to my cousin's house and Traphosa seemed all right at first, but quite suddenly she said she had a headache and lay down. When I went to see her, she did not know me. She started talking to Matron, as if she were there; she kept saying she was sorry and would she give her another chance. Then she called me and said she would come to town and do whatever I suggested. After a while, she seemed to be talking to the patients and saying that she was coming to make them all well. This went on and on and I was very frightened. When Matron appeared, I was so glad that she would do something for Traphosa that I forgot to say how sorry I was that we had run away. She was very kind to me and said that if I liked I could help to nurse Traphosa." Lena paused. "If she doesn't get better, it will be all my fault," she sobbed.

"Don't say that, Lena," said Truphena. "Matron told us that Doctor said Traphosa would get better. We think you are very brave to come back. I am sure you will make a good nurse and Traphosa will be very happy when she knows that you are looking after her."

Lena stopped crying and they all went in to lunch.

"I shall be on the same ward as you this afternoon," said Truphena. "Perhaps we can do some washing and cleaning together."

"That will be fun," said Lena.

Truphena looked at her and thought how much older she seemed than when she had arrived a few weeks ago. The shock of the accident and the responsibility of looking after Traphosa had made her grow up.

After lunch, Truphena and Lena put on their most stiffly starched aprons and caps and, looking as neat and clean as possible, went over to the hospital.

"Traphosa may have to have an operation," said Lena, "but she is in the Medical Ward at the moment because it is quieter than the Surgical. She will stay there until she recovers consciousness."

They reported to Sister, who welcomed them and said that they could start by cleaning the bedside lockers. They each took a basin and poured in some water and disinfectant, found some cloths and started working down either side of the ward. Traphosa's bed was on the side Truphena was doing. As she looked down at the unconscious face, Traphosa opened her eyes and a flicker of recognition seemed to come into them. Then she closed them again and sighed. Truphena walked over to Lena.

"Come over here," she said quietly. "I think Traphosa is coming round."

Lena walked over to the bed where her friend lay. Traphosa opened her eyes. This time she looked straight at Lena and smiled. Then she turned over and seemed to fall into a normal sleep.

"I must tell sister at once," said Lena, hardly able to keep back her excitement.

She ran out of the ward to Sister's little office. "Sister," she called, "I think Traphosa will be all right. She smiled at me and I'm sure she knew me."

"I'll come at once," said Sister.

She got up and walked quickly over to Traphosa.

"Yes, she seems to be sleeping naturally now. Listen to her breathing. Fetch a chair and sit by the bed; when she opens her eyes again, speak to her softly. Just say her name and ask her how she feels. Perhaps she will answer you. If she does, come and tell me."

Truphena went on washing the lockers and Lena sat by Traphosa's bed, anxiously watching her. In half an hour, she was rewarded. Traphosa opened her eyes and said, "Where am I?" She smiled when she saw Lena. "Am I at your house?" she asked.

"You are in hospital; there was an accident; you will be all right," answered Lena, hardly able to keep back the tears.

"Why are you crying?" asked Traphosa.

"I thought you were not going to get well," said Lena, "but now I know you will and I am so happy, I can't stop crying!"

Tears were now pouring down Lena's cheeks. Staff Nurse saw what was happening and called Sister. Sister came and bent over Traphosa.

"Don't send me away," cried Traphosa. "I don't quite remember what happened, but I know I ran away because I didn't want to do s.ome of the jobs on the wards, but now I don't mind and oh, really I do want to be a nurse! Will you take me back?"

"Don't get so excited," said Sister. "Matron has said that as soon as you are quite well again you can come back if you want to.

"Go back to sleep now; it is not good for you to talk too much. Lena will be here when you wake up and then you can have your little chat."

Lena helped her turn over and straightened out the bedclothes.

"I should like a drink, please," said Traphosa.

Lena fetched a feeding cup with a long spout and, lifting Traphosa's head gently, poured a few drops into her mouth.

"See what a good nurse your friend has become," said Sister watching approvingly.

Lena smiled. Traphosa closed her eyes and was asleep.

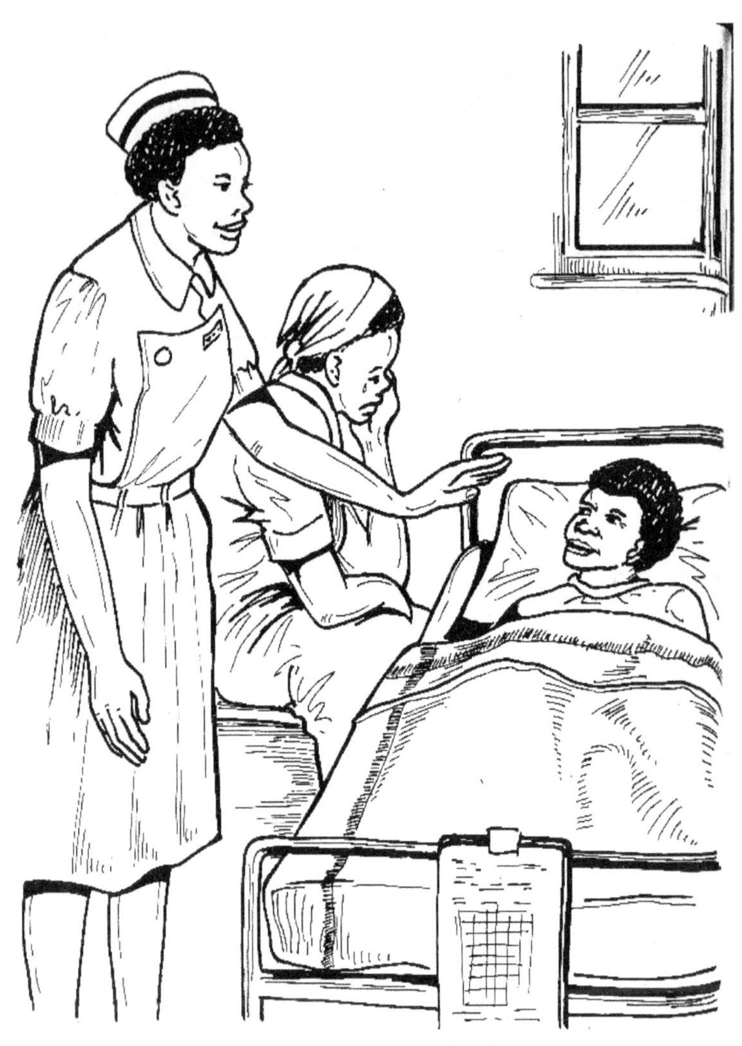

"Don't send me away," cried Traphosa.

As Truphena came off duty at five o'clock, she met Murimi coming out of the Men's Ward. Immediately she told him about Traphosa. "Isn't it wonderful that she will be all right?" she finished.

"It certainly is," he replied, "and it is also wonderful that she now really wants to be a nurse."

They walked out of the hospital in silence.

"Are you doing anything after tea?" asked Murimi.

"Not really," said Truphena shyly. "I suppose I ought to study my lecture notes."

"You can do that this evening," said Murimi "Meet me outside the Nurses' Home after tea and let's go for a walk."

Truphena thought for a moment. "Yes, I'd like to do that," she replied.

"In half an hour then," called Murimi gaily.

"In half an hour," she repeated.

Truphena went slowly upstairs and changed her uniform for a plain, yellow dress. She had made this just before she had received the letter to say she had been accepted at the hospital. She knew it fitted well and the colour suited her. She went down to tea, but found she could not eat a thing.

She felt almost sick with excitement. Murimi had never asked her to go out alone with him before. Always it had been with Mira and one of the other male nurses. Her mouth felt dry and she thought she would have nothing to say to him; then he would think she was dull and would not ask her ever again! Should she say she had a head-ache and send Mira to tell him she couldn't go? No, that would be silly; he knew she had been perfectly all right a few minutes ago. Should she ask Mira to come too? No, that would spoil it; she really wanted to be alone with Murimi. "I shall ask him about his home and if he has decided where to go when he has finished his training, then he will talk about himself and I needn't say much," thought Truphena. "I expect it will be all right when I am with him."

You look very nice," said Zipporah, who had just come in. "Going to meet your boy-friend?"

Truphena wished that Zipporah would not be quite so outspoken. She did not know how to answer, so she said nothing.

"Bring him for a game of tennis," said Zipporah, as she gulped down a cup of tea and three slices of bread and jam.

"I'm off now; be seeing you —perhaps," she added with a smile and ran up to the dormitory to change into tennis shorts.

Truphena's heart was beating so fast when she saw Murimi waiting for her that she thought he would be sure to hear it.

"Hallo," he called, as soon as he saw her. He held out his hand. "Let's go down to the river," he said. "There won't be too many people today; nearly everyone is going to watch the tennis players practising for the tournament.

Truphena took his hand and suddenly her heart seemed to beat more normally and her shyness left her. They walked down the path towards the river and Murimi began telling her about his afternoon on the ward. They talked a little about Lena and Traphosa and then Murimi asked her about her family. He was interested to know that Benaiah was doing well at school.

"Tell me about your family," said Truphena.

So Murimi told her about his widowed mother and his two older brothers, who were teachers. They had helped to pay for his schooling and were now paying for his two younger brothers and three sisters.

"I suppose that I ought to find a job to help as well," said Murimi. "Three and a half years is a long time to train without actually earning anything, but I have always wanted to be a dispenser. I want to go to a country district where the dispensary is the only means of medical aid for miles around; that is how I can best help my people."

He turned to Truphena. "Would you come with me?" he asked softly, taking both her hands and looking down at her.

They stood quite still for a few moments. The only noise was the sound of the wind in the trees, the rush of the river falling over the stones and the bird in the tree above them calling to its mates.

"Give me time to think about it," she said at last.

He kissed her gently. They turned and walked slowly back to the hospital, hand in hand.

Chapter 6

The Surprise

Truphena had now been given regular work on the wards. She was rapidly gaining experience and things that were so strange to her at first now seemed quite ordinary. She had learnt how to sweep and clean without spreading dust and germs, and how important it was for the comfort of the patients to give her attention to the smallest detail —a cheerful word to someone who looked sad or worried, or a pillow turned over; a hot water bottle to relieve an ache or pain. Such things made all the difference to a person's happiness; the atmosphere of the ward depended on the care the nurses gave to their patients.

Truphena had to get up early to be on the wards by a quarter-past seven. She helped the night staff to take temperatures, hand round breakfast trays and clean up before the regular day staff came on duty. She was now allowed the responsibility of giving medicines and, under the supervision of the ward Sister, she was learning to give injections. She realized the comfort a bed-bath gave to patients who were unable to get up. She could make a bed swiftly and was often praised for the neatness of her hospital corners!

At half-past nine Truphena and the other students left the wards and, after a short break for tea and bread, collected their books and went to the classroom for lectures. After lunch they were free for three afternoons a week; the other three were spent on practical work. At half-past four they went back on the wards until seven o'clock. Most Sundays they were off duty but, if they were needed, they had time off during the week instead.

Truphena spent most of her free time with Murimi. She told him all the little incidents that had happened during the day. She told him her troubles, too: how the new Staff nurse seemed to find fault with everything she did; how she had dropped a basin with a loud 'clang' just as the doctor was about to examine a patient. She told him the good things, too: how Sister had praised her for her quickness; how happy some of the patients seemed to be to see her. There was a growing friendship and understanding between them and she found peace in his company. After a difficult lecture, Murimi would explain things she did not understand; he seemed to grasp new facts easily and Sister Tutor often praised him for his clear answers to her questions.

Sometimes, on a Sunday, Truphena and Murimi would ask the cooks for some food and go out for the whole day. The surrounding countryside was very beautiful and they would climb to the top of the nearby hills and look down at the little houses nestling amongst the trees, each with its own plot of land. Murimi took pleasure in noticing the variety of crops that were grown besides the staple food.

"The people round here have a good mixed diet," he said once, "that is why they are so healthy. I shall not be needed so much here as in other places."

They would sit for a long time and listen to the sounds of the cattle lowing, the goats bleating and the birds singing. Such days were a joy to them both, and more and more Truphena felt that her future lay with Murimi. Yet, sometimes, a doubt would creep in and she resented the fact that he took it for granted that she would spend all her free time with him. Sometimes Murimi's friend, Onyango, would come along with Mira and those days would be full of fun and gaiety and not nearly so serious as the times Truphena spent alone with Murimi.

One evening, after the four of them had been out together, Mira said to Truphena, "Are you going to marry Murimi?"

For the first time, Truphena expressed her thoughts aloud. "I just don't know," she answered. "I feel contented in his company and he is so easy to talk to, but I feel I am missing something, although I don't quite know what. Sometimes I envy Zipporah and her medical student friend. They seem to have so much fun together. He comes along unexpectedly and Zipporah drops whatever she is doing and they go off laughing together. Sometimes they ask Matron's permission to go into the town for a dance. They both spend all their money for the month in a day and have nothing till the next lot of pocket money is given out. Murimi would never do anything like that — he is always so careful and never comes to take me out unless he has arranged it beforehand. We have never been into town because he says there is not much point spending money in that way when we have all we need here. Oh, I see his point, but just once in a while I wish he would do something exciting.

"Soon after we came here, he told me that he wanted to go to an isolated place as a dispenser and asked me to go with him. But I am not sure if I really want that sort of life. Not yet, anyway."

"The excitement you want would not last," said Mira softly. "I wish it was me that Murimi loved." She sighed deeply. Truphena looked at her.

"Oh, you poor thing," she said. "I had no idea you felt like that about Murimi. Is there anything I can do?"

"Nothing except, for my sake, do not hurt him," replied Mira.

Truphena said no more. That night she thought, "Murimi loves me and I don't know whether I love him or not. I think I do, but surely if I really loved him I shouldn't be frightened of feeling lonely away from here with him. I don't want to hurt him, but I can't decide yet."

The next day was a Sunday and Sister Tutor had promised them a suprise. She had told them all to be ready in the hall of the Nurses' Home at nine o'clock. They heard a bus pull up outside the door and then Sister Njau appeared, dressed in a smart blue suit.

"I have ordered the bus to take us out for the day," she said. "Rebecca, you and Truphena go to the kitchen and bring the boxes of food that you will see on the table. Murimi and Onyango, you can go too and help them to carry everything."

In a few moments the four of them staggered out, each with a large cardboard box. "If these are all full of food, we could stay out for a week!" remarked Murimi.

"It will soon disappear," said Sister Njau. "You will have good appetites in the fresh air!"

They stored the boxes near the driver's seat and away they went.

It was a lovely morning; the sun shone brightly and there was not a cloud in the sky. As they drove along, some of them sang softly. Looking out of the window, Truphena could see the outline of the distant mountain; it was very clear in the morning air. Murimi was sitting behind her.

"Look at the mountain," she said, pointing towards it.

"It is very beautiful," he answered. "Once, when I was at school, a party of us climbed right to the top. It was the most wonderful experience that I have ever had. On top, above the clouds, I felt at peace with the whole world, and beyond. Some day I shall climb it again."

After about an hour's drive, the bus stopped at a large farm. Murimi jumped down and opened the gate; the bus swung through and up the drive to the farmhouse. Sister Njau got out and knocked at the door. A friendly-looking man answered and invited them all into the house. They found themselves in a large living-room; the farmer's wife had laid out cups on the table and now she came into the room, carrying a teapot and a plate of homemade cakes.

"Help yourselves everyone," she said. "Then you shall see round the farm."

While they were having tea, the farmer's wife told Truphena that they had been at the farm for ten years. "I used to live in the city," she said, "and I felt very loney at first, but I soon started to take an interest in the animals and now I would rather live on the farm than anywhere else. My job is to look after the hens and young animals. I feed the calves when they are taken away from their mothers and care for any orphaned animals."

"Why should the calves be taken away from their mothers?" asked Truphena.

"Well, you see, if they are left to suck all the time the cows would not be milked. So we take them away and feed them at certain times of the day; as soon as they are old enough, we give them "cattle-cake' as well and that makes them grow very strong," explained the farmer's wife.

"Now for our tour," said the farmer, and he led them to a large shed. It was very clean and the walls were white-washed. Inside, there were thirty stalls. "This is where the cows are milked," said the farmer. "They give up to two gallons of milk each, every night and morning."

Truphena, whose father's cows barely gave two pints of milk a day, could hardly believe her ears.

"The cows are all milked by machine," he went on "This is what it is like." He showed them a round, steel container to which rubber tubes were attached. "These tubes fix on to the cows' udders and when the machinery is switched on, the milk is drawn automatically from the teats. You must come along one day, about four o'clock, and watch the milking.

"Let's go to the dairy," he said. They followed him into a building which, to Truphena, looked like a huge sluice. There were white tiles on the bottom half of the walls and everything looked as clean as it had to be in the operating theatre. The farmer explained how the milk was poured into containers straight from the milking- machines. "It is untouched by hand," he said proudly. "These containers are stood in others holding water heated to a certain temperature; the heat penetrates through and all the germs in the milk are killed; then it is poured directly into sterilized bottles, which are automatically sealed."

"Why don't you just boil the milk?" asked Mira.

"There are several reasons for that," answered the farmer. "The main reason is that although boiling makes milk perfectly safe to drink, it destroys certain vitamins; even more important, it alters the taste so much that many children won't drink it at all.

"Let's see the calves now," said the farmer. "Most people like to see them."

They followed him into another shed, where wide-eyed calves watched their movements and skipped into the corner of their pen when anyone tried to stroke them.

"Look, there are two in here," said Mira.

"Yes," said the farmer. "They are very young; in fact they were born only two days ago. I had to call the veterinary

"The cows are all milked by machine," said the farmer.

surgeon-that's an animal doctor-for the mother because I thought she would die. But she is all right now and the calves are fine, as you can see.

"Just before you go, take a look at the cows in this field," said the farmer, with pride. "They are a cross-bred variety and do very well here."

Truphena saw a fine, healthy herd grazing in the rich pasture, their coats, smooth and glossy, glinting in the sunshine.

It was time to go, so they thanked the farmer for showing them round and boarded the bus.

"Come and have tea with us sometime," called farmer's wife, who had come down in time to see them off.

"Thanks, we shall!" they called back. "Good-bye."

"That is one of the best farms in the district," said Sister Njau, as they drove away. "Very few are run as well as that. I wish we were nearer, then we should not have to boil our milk at the hospital."

They drove further into the country and then stopped and had their food. After a while, Sister suggested that they should all go for a walk.

"Don't get lost," she called after them, laughingly, "we should leave here at four o'clock."

Truphena found Murimi beside her as they wandered off. They started talking about the farm and Murimi said that one day all the farms in the country would be run like that. "In some parts of the country, people drink much more milk than they do here," he said. "They should be very healthy, but they get ill through a germ in the milk. If only they would boil their milk, the germs would be killed. I should like to go to one of those areas; I feel I could do such a lot to help the people there."

He told Truphena of his dreams and ambitions and as she listened, she realized what a wonderful person he was. "He is too good for me," she thought. "He is always thinking of how he can help others; he never thinks of himself."

On the way home, the mountain was just visible in the light of the setting sun. Everyone was quiet as they travelled back towards the hospital. Then Murimi's deep voice was heard, singing of the beauty and peace to be found on the mountain peak, above the clouds.

Chapter 7

Night Duty

Truphena had passed well in both the written and practical parts of the Preliminary Examination. Lena, much to her surpise, had come second in Practical Nursing; Traphosa would have to sit her written papers again, in three months time, as she had not been able to catch up with all the lectures she had missed; Rebecca had come top, tying with Murimi.

They still attended lectures, but now they spent much more time on the wards. One day, after class, Sister Tutor asked Truphena and Mira to stay behind.

"I have very good reports from the sisters about your work on the wards," she said. "How would you like to go on night duty?"

Truphena and Mira looked at each other. This showed that Sister trusted them. Night duty meant taking more responsibility and they would not be asked to do that unless Sister felt sure they were ready for it.

"I should like that," said Truphena.

"Yes, I should too," said Mira.

They tried to appear calm, but really they were both very excited.

"Then you may start tonight," said Sister. "Truphena, you will go to the Children's Ward, and Mira, you win go to the Women's Medical. You start duty at a quarter-past nine and stay until the day staff takes over in the morning. A Staff Nurse will be in charge of the ward and Night Sister will come round from time to time to see that everything is all right. You will have a meal before you go on duty and take sandwiches to have during the night.

You can make tea in the Duty Room. Try to get some sleep this afternoon or you will be very tired indeed by tomorrow morning. You can move your things over to the Day Room, where the night nurses sleep, or you can stay in your own dormitory —it is up to you."

At lunch, Truphena and Mira planned the rest of the day. They decided to go for a walk, lay out their uniforms, have tea and then try to sleep until eight o'clock. They could then have their meal and be over at the hospital in good time. They decided to move to the Day Room the following morning.

Truphena set her alarm and by five o'clock she and Mira were in bed; but they did not feel at all sleepy! They lay very still so as not to disturb each other until, at seven o'clock, Truphena threw back the bed-clothes and got out of bed. Mira sat up. "I can't sleep," she said.

"I haven't slept at all," said Truphena. "If I had known that you were awake, I should have got up before."

"I thought you were asleep, or I shouldn't have been so quiet," said Mira.

They both laughed.

"Let's dress and go downstairs and do our knitting — it's no good staying here. I expect we shall be tired enough tomorrow afternoon," said Truphena.

"By the way, I wonder if we are allowed to take our knitting with us on night duty?"

"I meant to ask Sister that," said Mira. "Let's see if there is anyone downstairs who knows."

They dressed and went down to the sitting-room. No one there had been on night duty. They went along to the games room and found Zipporah and her friends practising for the tournament. "I thought you two were going on night duty," she said. "You should be sleeping."

"We couldn't sleep," said Truphena. "We want to know if we can take our knitting on the wards?"

"You can take what you like, but Sister usually finds a hundred and one jobs for you to do. If you have really finished everything and all the patients are asleep, you sometimes manage to get some knitting done."

"I just want to finish the sleeve of my cardigan," said Truphena. "I think I'll take it, hopefully. It is cold at night now that the rainy season has come; I wish I had finished it before."

Soon it was time for their meal and then Truphena and Mira walked over to the hospital. It seemed strange to be going on duty when most of their world would soon be thinking of going to bed.

All was very quiet as they entered the hospital. Truphena said good-bye to Mira at the door of the Medical Ward and walked over to the Children's Ward.

The lights were dimmed but she could just see the occupants of each little cot. They all appeared to be sleeping peacefully. She went to report to the Staff Nurse.

"Is this your first time on night duty?" asked the Staff Nurse.

Truphena said that it was. "You will get used to the strangeness after a few nights," said Staff Nurse kindly. "There is one little boy I am worried about. Will you bring a chair and sit with him for a while? I have these reports to write up."

She walked over to the cot in the corner. "This is Eleeja," she said. "He only came in this afternoon and Dr. Njoroge says he is very ill. He is coming to see him tonight about eleven o'clock, but I have to call him before if the little chap seems worse."

Truphena took a chair and sat down quietly beside Eleeja. She put her hand gently on his head; she expected him to feel hot and feverish but, instead, he felt rather cold. His breathing was slow and sometimes seemed to stop altogether. Every now and then he gave a little moan; otherwise he lay quite still.

She felt his pulse —it was slow and irregular.

After about half an hour, another nurse came to relieve Truphena. Just then there was a loud cry from the far end of the room, followed by shrieks of "Mumma, Mumma." Truphena rushed over and picked up a small girl. The child stopped crying for a moment and looked up at Truphena. "You're not mumma," she said and immediately started crying again. Staff Nurse rushed in and took her from Truphena.

"Hush," she said to the frightened child, "your mumma will be here tomorrow.

The little girl gradually became quite and fell asleep. Staff Nurse laid her gently back in her cot.

"Three children have to be woken up for medicine," said Staff Nurse to Truphena. She pointed out who they were and Truphena helped her measure out the correct dosage. She watched as Staff Nurse picked up one of the children and, hardly waking him at all, gently opened his mouth and poured in the medicine.

Just before eleven o'clock Dr. Njoroge came into the ward and asked how Eleeja was. He went over and felt his pulse, looking very grave. He said something to Staff Nurse, who disappeared for a few moments and returned with a syringe and a small bottle. Dr. Njoroge filled the syringe carefully and injected some liquid into the child's arm.

"That should keep his heart beating," he said, "but you must call me if his pulse becomes weaker. We may have to call the 'Flying Doctor Service' in the morning to take him to the National Hospital."

When he had gone, Staff Nurse told Truphena she could make some tea and have her sandwiches. Truphena went into the Duty Room and put on the kettle. She was beginning to feel sleepy. She wondered how Mira was getting on and who else was on night duty. Her thoughts turned to Murimi —was he asleep? Perhaps he was on night duty too; she had forgotten to find out. She would ask him in the morning. She drank her tea and felt better. She pulled aside the curtains; the night was very dark. There was no moon and the clouds had covered up the stars. Suddenly she felt lonely.

Staff Nurse came in. "I think Eleeja is getting worse," she said. "Come and look at him. We shall have to decide whether or not to call the Doctor."

("It was amazing how differently you were treated on night duty," thought Truphena, "not like a Junior Nurse at all.")

Truphena bent over the little boy and felt his pulse. It was slow, but not so slow as it had been when she had first arrived on the ward.

"He is better than he was when I was sitting with him," she said.

"I do hope he lives through the night," said Staff Nurse. "If we can have him flown to the National Hospital in the morning, the specialists there might be able to do something for him."

"What happened to him?" asked Truphena.

"We don't know exactly," answered Staff Nurse. "His mother said that he had fallen and hit his head; Doctor thinks his brain may be damaged."

"What shall I do now?" asked Truphena. She felt that if she was not kept busy she would feel sleepy again.

"There are some mackintoshes to wash in the sluice," said Staff Nurse, "and then you can tidy the medicine cupboards."

Truphena went into the sluice and found a pile of mackintoshes waiting to be rinsed and powdered. The other nurse came in and said she would give her a hand. "Of course, we use more of these in the Children's Ward than anywhere else in the hospital," she said, "but I like working here best, don't you?"

Truphena replied that she was not sure which ward she preferred, but she was looking forward to going in the theatre. They chatted away and, in no time at all, the clean mackintoshes were lying over the wooden racks.

"Now, let's clean out the cupboards," said Truphena.

"All right," said the nurse. "I can see that you really enjoy working!"

They turned out one cupboard and were going to start on the another, when Sister looked round the door. "Good evening, Nurses," she said. "How are you getting on?"

"Very well—thank you—we are cleaning out the cupboards," said Truphena.

"Have you a cup of tea to spare?" asked Sister.

Truphena poured out one for her. It was rather cold, but Sister drank it gratefully.

"Keep busy," she said, as she left them. "I shall come round again during the night to look at Eleeja."

Another hour passed. Then, suddenly, Staff Nurse came rushing into the sluice.

"I must call Dr. Njoroge at once," she said.

Truphena offered to go although she was rather scared to go out alone on such a dark night. Staff Nurse gave her a torch and told her where the Doctor's house was.

As Truphena went out of the hospital, she noticed that the heavy clouds had passed over and now there was a clear, starlit sky. She reached the Doctor's house and knocked on the door. There was no reply. She knocked louder. This time a sleepy voice called out, "Who is it?"

"Please, will Dr. Njoroge come to the Children's Ward as soon as possible," she said. "Staff Nurse thinks that Eleeja is worse."

Truphena heard a muffled sound and a few moments later Dr. Njoroge appeared, fastening his trousers hurriedly over his pyjamas. Together they hurried over to the hospital.

"Do you think he will be all right?" she could not help asking.

"I really don't know," answered Dr. Njoroge. "I have never seen a case quite like his before. If he shows no improvement by morning, we shall definitely send him to the National Hospital."

"If he goes, I wish that I could go with him," said Truphena, half aloud.

"Perhaps you will," replied Dr. Njoroge. "Such things have happened before."

The sky had clouded over again and the stars were completely hidden. As they reached the hospital huge drops of rain began to fall and, as they entered the ward, there was a brilliant flash, followed by a crash of thunder that seemed to shake the whole building. Three of the children awoke and started crying. Rather to Truphena's surprise, the others remained fast asleep.

Sister had come into the ward to help quiet the frightened children. Dr. Njoroge went over to Eleeja and listened to his heart.

"Please bring a syringe; we must give him another injection," he said to Staff Nurse. She brought a syringe and bottle.

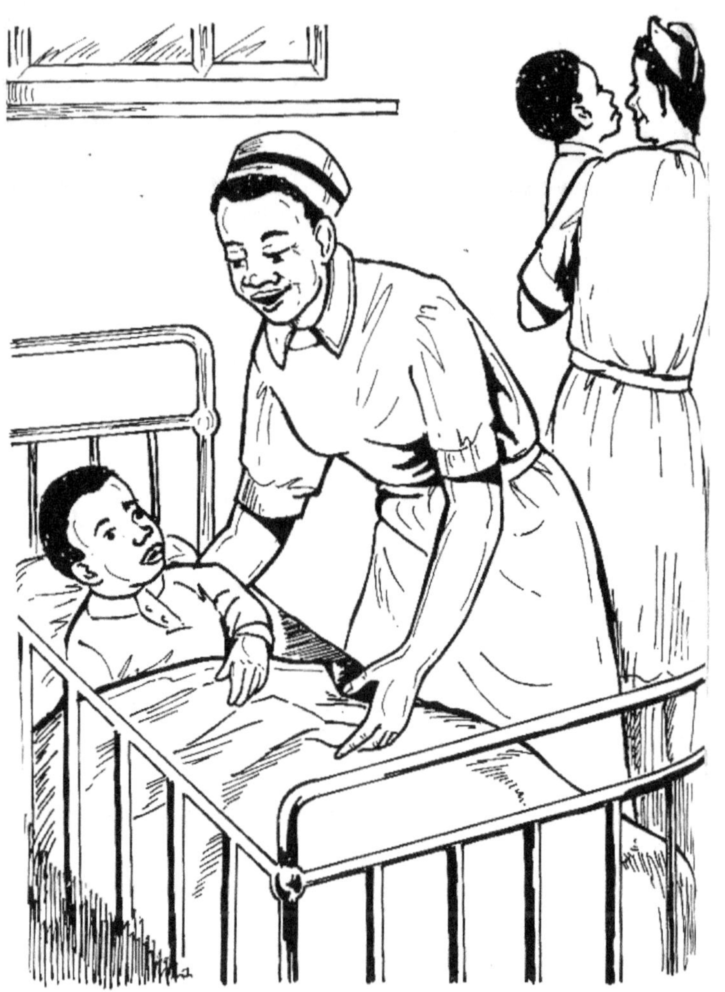

Sister had come into the ward to help quiet the frightened children.

"You give it this time," he said. "I want to keep listening to his heart."

After a few minutes he stood up. "Make some tea, Nurse," he said to Truphena. "I think I had better stay here the rest of the night."

About four o'clock in the morning, the storm was at its height. The lightning lit up the long ward and the thunder resounded round the walls. The wind became more violent and a tree crashed with a great roar. Several children woke and their crying woke the others. The nurses tried to comfort first one, then another. Truphena thought she would never forget her first night duty; the raging storm, the crying children and the unconscious, silent one in their midst.

As dawn broke the gale subsided and the awakened children dozed off into an exhausted sleep. By 6:30 the wind had dropped and, when Truphena pulled back the curtains, she saw a clear, pale blue sky. The lawns were covered with fallen leaves and the pretty flower beds looked bruised and battered. A tree had fallen across the drive, just missing the end of the hospital.

At half-past seven the day staff arrived and Night Sister suggested that they should let the children sleep for another hour and have their breakfast later.

Eleeja was still alive, still unconscious. Dr. Njoroge said he would try to radio the National Hospital. He told Truphena to go and have some breakfast, but not to go to bed in case she was needed.

As she was walking over to the Home, she met Zipporah. "Did you get any knitting done?" she asked.

"I forgot to take it in the end," Truphena answered, "and I never even noticed!"

Chapter 8

A Wonderful Adventure

Waves of sleep came over Truphena as she slowly sipped her second cup of tea. Mira came and sat down beside her. "Did you have a good night?" she asked.

Not wanting to be rude to her friend, Truphena said, "Do you mind if I tell you about it later? I feel too tired to talk much at the moment. How did your night go?"

"Oh, nothing much happened," said Mira. "The storm woke a few people. We made them hot, milky drinks and they soon went off to sleep again. I even had a little nap myself."

A nurse came into the room and, going straight up to Truphena, handed her a note. Truphena opened it and, as she read, her tiredness left her. It said, "The Flying Doctor Services plane will land in two hours time. Doctor has asked if you can look after Eleeja on the journey. I give you my permission to go." It was signed "Matron".

She handed the note to Mira, who could hardly believe her eyes! They went upstairs and, as if in a dream, Truphena pushed a few things into her bag. Then she went across to the hospital and along to the Children's Ward. No one would have realized that they had had such a restless night. Most of them were sitting up and eating a large breakfast. Eleeja lay in the corner cot, not knowing what was going on around him.

After some time, Truphena heard the low throb of the plane. She looked out of the window and saw a black speck in the distance coming towards the hospital. Sister came in and wrapped Eleeja in a large blanket. Truphena picked him up in her arms; a nurse took her bag and followed her to the waiting car. Dr. Njoroge himself drove her the short way to the airstrip. The plane circled once and made a perfect landing; it taxied to the end of the runway and returned to where Truphena and Dr. Njoroge were standing.

The pilot opened the tiny door and heaved himself out. He had a few words with Dr. Njoroge who introduced Truphena. Dr. Njoroge held Eleeja as the pilot helped Truphena into the plane, then she took the unconscious child on her knee. Dr. Njoroge handed her a letter. "This is for the Doctor," he said. "Good-bye —and good flying!"

Truphena tried the door to see that it was properly closed. "Don't worry about that," said the pilot.

"Don't worry! We're supposed to be coming too!" was Truphena's spirited reply.

The pilot laughed. "I don't mean that," he explained. "I have a switch to control the doors. I don't want to lose my passengers! Now fasten that safety belt round you — no, like this." (He showed her.) "Hold tight to your patient as we take off."

Truphena looked relieved and tried to relax. The pilot checked his instruments and started up the engine. With a roar the propeller whirled round so fast that Truphena could not see the separate blades; the noise seemed deafening as the plane sped along the short runway. Suddenly they were in the air. Dr. Njoroge, standing beside his car, seemed like a toy figure, as they rose higher into the sky; the hospital, with its neatly laid-out gardens and tennis court, looked like a child's model.

As the plane rose higher, Truphena had a queer feeling in her stomach; there was a buzzing in her ears and she felt as if she was going to be sick. The pilot looked at her. "Swallow hard," he said firmly.

She swallowed and at once felt better. The plane straightened out.

"After a few take-offs, you get used to that feeling," he said. "I always find the moment I leave the ground the most exciting. Don't you think it is peaceful up here?"

Truphena agreed. She looked at Eleeja and saw he was no worse.

"I hope we get him there in time and that the doctors at the National Hospital can do something for him," she said.

"We shall be there in less than two hours," said the pilot. "If you had gone by road, it would have taken at least eight hours, probably longer, as the roads are very bad because of the storm last night."

"Do you fly when there is a storm?" asked Truphena.

"We don't like to. In fact, we wouldn't start in a bad storm and, if we see one ahead when we are in the air, we can usually go round it or at least avoid the worst part of it."

Truphena could not understand how you could go round a storm, but she said nothing. There were so many things she did not understand, but it was noisy and she had to shout for the pilot to hear her, so she decided not to ask too many questions.

"Look down now," said the pilot. "You will see how the country changes as we fly over this ridge of hills."

Truphena looked down and saw they were leaving the pattern of green fields behind and were flying over a range of bare-looking hills. The plane rose higher and, every now and then, jerked up and down. She had that queer feeling in her inside again. Suddenly, there was a big bump and she looked at the pilot, feeling scared.

"Don't worry," he said. "These bumps are caused by air currents —they often happen when we fly over high ground, even on the calmest days."

They flew over the hills and she was amazed at the difference in the country. Instead of little huts surrounded by plots of cultivated land, there was a vast area of — nothing. She could not describe it any other way. For miles and miles there was dry, brownish-grey scrub. There was not a hut to be seen.

"Doesn't anyone live here?" asked Truphena. "What a lot of land. It looks as if it never rains."

"Quite a few people do live here," answered the pilot, "but they don't cultivate the land in the same way as the people round your way; they keep cattle and wander from place to place in order to find grazing for them. There is not much more than a few inches of rain a year here and you don't see a cloud in the sky for months on end. We shall fly a little lower and, if you look carefully, you will see groups of huts inside strong thorn fences. The huts are not very large because the people move about so much that they don't collect many things. Sometimes, I envy these people," he added. "We have too many possessions and when we move, we have such a lot of trouble packing up everything. However, it is part of modern life and I suppose we must accept it."

"Are there any hospitals in this area?" she asked after a while.

"There is a very small one about eighty miles from here and there are one or two dispensaries, but many more are needed."

Truphena's thoughts immediately turned to Murimi. This was the sort of place where he wanted to come. She wondered if he had ever been to this part of the country. She looked forward to telling him about it. "If I marry him," she thought, "I shall have to live in a place like this."

"Would you like to live here?" she asked the pilot.

He was silent for a moment. She waited for his reply, and all at once it seemed terribly important.

"I don't think so," he said slowly, a frown on his handsome face. "I love to visit these parts and I like the people but somehow, the simple life doesn't completely satisfy me any more. I could go back for a while, but I would soon long for the lights of the town, the shops, the people and the life of the city. No, I should not want to live here —I should be lonely."

"You said 'go back'," said Truphena. "Did you live here once?"

"Yes," answered the pilot. "These are my people, but my father sent me to school in the town. I managed to pass all my exams and was then accepted to train as a pilot. I go back to visit my people quite often. I am lucky to have this job, because I am not completely cut off from my relatives; they live near the little hospital I told you about."

The hot sun shone through the window of the plane and made Truphena feel sleepy. She dozed off, to be woken by a loud, crackling noise. She saw the pilot turn a handle near the roof and lift a speaker from the stand at his side. "This is the National Hospital, go ahead."

She heard a distorted voice say, "Z for Zebra, A for Antelope, B for Bush —this is pilot Ngaywa speaking. I shall be landing at 11:55 and request ambulance to take nurse and patient to National Hospital."

"National Hospital here —message received — ambulance will be waiting at airport and hospital ready to receive patient."

The pilot replaced the receiver. They flew on and on.

Truphena thought she had never known anything so

beautiful as the bright blue sky above and the changing country below.

"We can see three lakes from here," said the pilot.

He pointed ahead and Truphena could see a large expanse of shining water; in another direction she could see two smaller ones.

"Do many people live near the lakes?" asked Truphena.

"Yes, a great many do now," answered the pilot. "A few years ago, the Government sent officers to help to set up a large fishing industry."

She looked at him admiringly. "How do you know about all these things?" she asked.

"Well, I go round to so many different places and I often have to spend a night or two away from home. I find that people enjoy talking about things that are happening in their district; and, of course, living in a town you get to know what is happening in different parts of the country."

Truphena thought how wonderful he was. He was so easy to talk to and she had not felt shy for a moment.

"You can see the road down there," said the pilot.

Truphena looked and saw a winding murram road stretching through the countryside. "Look, there's a train —I can see the railway track near the road," she said excitedly. "Oh, it does look tiny!"

Pilot Ngaywa was delighted that he had such an interested and attractive companion. He asked her about her work at the hospital and how long she had been training. She told him why she had decided to become a nurse and about some of the hospital staff and students. For some reason, she did not mention Murimi! Eleeja was beginning to feel heavy on her lap; he seemed no worse, but she would be thankful when she had handed him over safely to the National Hospital.

Pilot Ngaywa was delighted that he had such an interesting and attractive companion.

"It won't be long now before we land," said the pilot, "I am going to call the airport in a few minutes."

Truphena saw that the country had changed again. It was flat and much greener. She could see the glinting roofs of the little houses, cultivated fields and cattle.

"We shall not fly over the city," said the pilot, "but you will see part of it, on your right, as we approach the airport."

He picked up the radio telephone by his side and wound up the aerial.

"City airport —go ahead," said an unknown voice.

"Z for Zebra, A for Antelope, B for Bush requests permission to land," said the pilot.

"Circle twice and call again," came the reply.

"Listen and you will hear other aircraft asking to land and being given instructions," the pilot explained to Truphena. "That is the control tower, where the voice is coming from." He pointed to a tall, white building. "All the runways are tarmacked here and very long —a change from the little strip at Lakimu! Now you can see the city."

Truphena saw miles and miles of buildings —all the green fields seemed to have been swallowed up by red brick. She could not imagine what it would be like to live in such a place.

"Do you live amongst all those buildings?" she asked.

"No," answered the pilot. "I live near the airport and there the houses have large gardens round them; although it is only about half an hour by car to the city centre. I have the best of both worlds!"

The pilot radioed again, and this time was given permission to land.

"Swallow hard as we go down," he said to Truphena. "That will take away the popping in your ears —and hold on to your little patient."

The plane lost height and Truphena thought the ground was rushing up to meet them. Once again, she had that sinking sensation in her stomach. She swallowed and held tightly to her precious bundle. With a slight bump, the wheels touched down on the runway and the plane sped like a racing car for a few hundred yards. The pilot slowed down and taxied back to the hangar.

Truphena could see the ambulance waiting. As the pilot opened the door and climbed stiffly out of the plane, the ambulance driver came towards them.

"Had a good trip?" he asked.

"Oh, yes, thank you," said Truphena.

He took Eleeja from her. "So this is the little chap, is it? How has he been on the way?"

"He has been unconscious all the time, but I don't think he's any worse for the journey," said Truphena.

"We'll soon have him in hospital. I'll lay him down on the stretcher and you can jump in beside him," said the driver.

The pilot walked with them to the ambulance.

"Thank you so much," said Truphena.

"It was a pleasure," he answered. "I hope Eleeja gets better. Perhaps I shall see you on another of my trips."

They said good-bye and Truphena quickly climbed up beside Eleeja.

They were soon racing along the road to the hospital and, within half an hour, the ambulance pulled up in front of a large building, outside an entrance marked 'Casualty'. A Sister was waiting and took Eleeja before Truphena had time to lift him down herself.

"The Surgeon is ready," she said. "Just sit in the waiting-room a moment, please."

Truphena handed her the letter she had been given. "This is for the doctor," she said.

Truphena was nearly asleep when someone came to take her to the canteen for a meal. Then she was shown into a little room with a long couch and told she could rest until it was time to go for the train. Everything had been arranged, she was told. A taxi would take her to the station at this end and another would meet her at Longaru, the nearest stop to Lakimu.

Too tired to question anything, she lay down on the couch and fell into a deep sleep.

Chapter 9

Finals

Work became all important as the time for the final examination drew near. The girls even gave up their knitting and sewing and spent their evenings studying.

Every morning they worked in pairs for an hour, doing what they needed to practise most. Truphena and Mira worked together, bandaging each other's arms and legs and putting splints in the correct positions. They made up beds in different ways for patients suffering from various complaints; they 'bed-bathed' Penima, the model; they asked each other questions about bones and found them on Johnson the skeleton. They worked with other students, in threes and fours, to practise lifting 'helpless' patients; they fed each other, lying down, with special cups.

At last the day of the written examination arrived. This they were to do in their own classroom. The Oral and Practical were to be held the following day at Longaru.

At eight o'clock the students were all sitting at their desks in the classroom. Each desk was well separated from the others and on each were several sheets of foolscap paper and a clean sheet of blotting paper. They sat quietly, waiting for Sister Njau.

"How different this room seems now from the friendly place it usually is," thought Truphena. "It looks quite unfamiliar."

She glanced round the room. The models, bed, cot and trolleys had been cleared away and it seamed strange and bare. Everyone was looking anxious, except Rebecca, who appeared as calm as she always did, no matter what she was doing.

Nothing ever worried or hurried Rebecca; Truphena had often watched her on the wards, soothing an excitable patient. Once there was a young man, almost frantic with terror, because he was to have a serious operation. Rebecca had been sent to prepare him and, as she went about her duties explaining why she did everything, he became perfectly calm and told her he was no longer afraid. Truphena wished she was more like Rebecca and kept her in mind as an example.

No one spoke as Sister Tutor came into the room with a large envelope. She broke the seal and handed each student a question paper. She set the clock to exactly 8:15 and told them to begin. Truphena wrote her name on the first sheet of foolscap, sat back and read through the examination paper.

Question I. Describe the functions of the skin. "I know that one," she thought. Question II. Draw a diagram to show the circulation of the blood. "I wish my drawings were neater; I can do that, but I should prefer to write about it. Let's see what the other questions are about."

There was one on the different kind of foodstuffs needed by the body; another on the digestive system; one on how the brain and spinal cord are protected and several short questions about the skeleton, muscles and tissues and respiration.

Truphena carefully chose the questions which she thought she could do best and settled down to write. The time went by so quickly that she did not realize how long she had been writing until Sister Tutor said, "You have another half hour."

"Just twenty minutes for the last question," thought Truphena. "I must leave time to read over my answers. I wish I had not spent quite so long over the diagram but, still, it is better than the ones I usually do, and certainly much neater!"

The last question, on how to recognize abnormal breathing, she did fairly quickly and left herself nearly ten minutes to read through her papers. She had not quite finished before Sister said, "Stop writing now!" They laid down their pens, tied their papers together and waited for Sister to collect them.

As they went out of the door, the relief that the exam was over showed in a rush of talk. "Did you do that one?" "I was lucky. I studied up the circulation only last night." "I forgot to put something in and I only remembered when Sister told us to stop writing." No one was really listening to anyone else. Truphena suddenly realized she was terribly hungry and she felt she could not talk to anybody until she had had her lunch.

In the afternoon there was a shorter written exam on Practical Nursing and First Aid. Truphena found this quite easy and, looking round at the others, she thought that they all felt the same way. Faces looked far less strained than in the morning.

Sister Tutor told the students that they should all have an early night, as the bus would be ready at half-past seven the next morning to take them to town for their oral exams.

Truphena worked until ten o'clock that evening, and then went to bed; but she could not sleep. Things she wished she had written in her paper kept coming into her mind and in the end she began to wonder if she had written anything sensible at all! She kept sleeping and waking and was glad when it was time to get up.

In spite of her restless night, she felt wide awake and alert. She washed and dressed quickly and had finished her breakfast before most of the others appeared. She had a last glance at her notes and then it was time to board the bus.

Sister Tutor accompanied them and when they arrived at Longaru Hospital, she found out where they were to go. Just after nine o'clock, they were sitting in the waiting-room. The Hospital Sister Tutor came and gave Sister Njau a list of students and the order in which they were to go. Promptly at half-past nine there was a light knock on the door and a smart young girl, in a well-fitting green dress, appeared and said that Mr. Ngugi was ready for the first candidate.

Sister had already read out the list of names. Rebecca was first, so she followed the girl out of the room.

"That is the Surgeon's secretary," said Sister Njau. "She is young to have such a responsible job."

There were three other students before it was Truphena's turn. She felt nervous as she knocked timidly at the great man's door. Mr. Ngugi had occasionally given a lecture to the students and once he had visited the Surgical Ward when she had been on duty. He had seemed a very superior person and she did not know how she would be able to speak to him normally. She thought that she would forget everything when he asked her a question.

"Come in," said a deep voice. She walked into the room.

Mr. Ngugi was busily writing something at his desk. He looked up and smiled at Truphena, a kind, friendly smile, and began asking her how she had enjoyed her training. He made her feel that he was more interested in her than in anyone else in the world; in fact this was partly true as, whenever he spoke to anybody, he gave them his whole attention and thought about nothing else.

After a few minutes, Truphena was completely at ease. Mr. Ngugi sensed this and began his questioning. He handed her a bone and asked her what it was and where it was found. "Good," he said, when she had answered.

He took it away and handed her another. Then he asked her a few questions about the lungs and heart and lastly why it was important to have everything sterile when dressing a wound after an operation. He made her feel that she knew much more than she actually did, and she walked out of the room feeling very happy.

Rebecca had already been in to see the Physician. Patiently, and full of confidence, Truphena waited her turn. She knocked at the door. There was no answer. She waited a moment and then opened the door slowly and peeped round.

"Wait a moment!" roared a furious voice. Terrified, Truphena withdrew. Her confidence left her and she felt sure she would fail.

"Come in now," roared the same voice.

"Oh, well, they can't all be like Mr. Ngugi, I suppose," thought Truphena, "and I was wrong about him at first." She crept into the room.

"I'm not going to eat you, girl" said Dr. Abuor, more kindly. "I was on the phone to Majimbo, two hundred and fifty miles away and I could hardly hear what they were saying."

Truphena breathed a sigh of relief; perhaps this was not going to be so bad after all.

"Now, how do you check that you are giving the correct amount of medicine to the patient?" he began.

"This might seem a simple question, but it's very important one, don't you agree?"

Truphena thought of her normal procedure on the wards and hoped it was correct. "I look at the patient's notes; make sure it is the correct time to give the medicine and I read the lable on the bottle," she replied.

He looked at her and waited. She knew that he wanted her to say something more, but her mind was completely blank. She stared in front of her.

"How do you know the patient won't throw the medicine into the flower vase or something?" asked Dr. Abuor.

"Oh, I stay with the patient until he has taken it," answered Truphena.

"What causes malnutrition?" was the next question. Truphena knew the answer to this well, but somehow Dr. Abuor made her feel nervous and she did not answer quickly or remember everything without prompting. After a few more questions about the need of the body for vitamins, he told her, much to her surprise, that she had answered very well!

She went back to Sister Njau and the others. She had a sudden longing to talk to Murimi, but the men were altogether in a corner, so she went and sat by Mira. Mira had done well with Mr. Ngugi and was now waiting to see Dr. Abuor. Truphena told her that he was a rather frightening person, but that he did not really mean to be and hoped that Mira would answer better than she had done.

Lena was nearly in tears; she said she had riot remembered anything when Mr. Ngugi had questioned her, although he had been so kind and tried to help her; with Dr. Abuor it had been even worse. She said she knew she had failed. Rebecca tried to cheer her up by reminding her how well she had done in the Preliminary Practical. Sister Njau noted with approval, the quiet way in which Rebecca made Lena cheerful again. Lena would make a good nurse if only she would not get so upset over things; she had nursed Traphosa devotedly for long hours, but once away from the wards her self-confidence deserted her. If she did pass her exams, it would help her very much.

At last they had all finished and were taken to the dining-room for lunch. There was not much time before their Practical Nursing Exam. They were to work in pairs. Truphena and Mira happily found themselves together. The Matron and Sister Tutor of Longaru Hospital were in charge. Matron was very tall and severe- looking, but she had great charm and was the kind of person everyone wanted to please. Immediately, Truphena felt a great respect for her and hoped for her praise.

First of all they were asked to make up a bed for an imaginary patient coming back from the operating theatre; this they had practised many times and could do swiftly and well. Then Truphena had to bandage Mira as if she had a head injury; Mira had to fix splints on Truphena's legs; Truphena was then asked to lay up a trolley for the ward Sister to do a wound dressing and Mira had to explain for what all the instruments and bowls were used. A few questions about taking tempera-tures, pulse and blood pressure and they were told they could go.

Back in the waiting-room, Truphena and Mira talked in whispers about the exam; they were feeling fairly pleased with themselves and thought they had done reasonably well. At last, everyone had finished and they trooped down to the dining-room for a welcome cup of tea before the bus took them back to Lakimu.

Truphena was then asked to lay up a trolley for the ward Sister to do a wound dressing and Mira had to explain what all the instruments and bowls were used for.

At first, they were silent, feeling rather flat and exhausted after the long day. Then Murimi started singing quietly; gradually the others joined in and soon the whole bus load, including Sister Njau, were singing happily. By the time they reached the hospital, they were in good spirits. The next day was Sunday, and for a whole day, they agreed to forget their exams.

Chapter 10

The Decision

The day of the Graduation Ceremony arrived at last. No rain was expected and a temporary platform had been built in the garden of the Nurses' Home. Mr. Ngugi was to come to present the certificates. The girls assembled at two o'clock in their new light blue uniforms, their caps and aprons starched to perfection; the men wore new white coats.

It was now six weeks after the Finals. Two weeks ago, they had heard, to their relief, that they had all passed, even Lena, despite her fears! Murimi came top, Rebecca second and Truphena third. Some had decided to stay in the hospital, others were found posts elsewhere. There was no lack of work for them, almost anywhere in the country. Several times, Murimi had asked Truphena if she would go with him to Takima and each time she had put off the decision. Very soon, she must make up her mind.

Parents were arriving and Truphena caught sight of her mother with Benaiah and several of her younger brothers and sisters; she waved to them as they took their places in the guests' enclosure. Afterwards there was to be a tea party in the Nurses' Home.

At half-past two, a car drew up; Mr. Ngugi got out and walked slowly towards the platform. Matron went to meet him, shook hands and led him to his seat.

It was a perfect day. The sun shone in a cloudless sky; the birds sang and a slight breeze rustled the leaves of the trees. The House Surgeon was present, the Hospital Administrator and most of the sisters. The local M.P. was the guest of honour and sat beside Mr. Ngugi.

The Hospital Administrator gave a short speech and introduced Matron. Matron recalled the early days of the hospital, before there was electric lighting, and also the history of the Nurses Training School. She introduced Mr. Ngugi.

Mr. Ngugi said how glad he was that the students had been so well trained that he had not had to fail anybody in the examination; that made his coming to present the certificates a very happy occasion indeed. He then congratulated Murimi for being top student. "I hear you are going to Takima," he said. "You have made a good decision and will serve your country well. This hospital should be proud of you."

The names of the other students were read out as, one by one, they went up for their certificates. When they were all back in their places the M.P. gave a short speech, congratulating the new nurses and saying that they had chosen a noble profession; he hoped they would enjoy their work, wherever they happened to be.

Then the ceremony was over and the nurses were told that they could take their parents in to tea.

Truphena ran to find her mother. She gave her a big hug and her little brothers and sisters crowded round and admired her new uniform. "Don't dirty it," said Truphena. "I have to wear it on duty this evening. My others have not been made yet!"

"Benaiah, come and meet Matron," said Truphena. "You are the cause of my being here."

Benaiah hung back. "Come on," she said, "just for me." He could not resist that appeal and went with his sister.

"This is my brother, Benaiah, Matron," said Truphena, when she had found her in the crowd. "I should like you to meet him, because if it were not for him I probably shouldn't be here."

The names of the students were read out as, one by one, they went up for their certificates.

"Good afternoon, Benaiah," said Matron. "What are you doing now?"

"I am still at school," said Benaiah, "but if I am good enough at science, I hope to go to the University and become a doctor."

"That is good to hear," said Matron. "I see you are becoming quite a medically-minded family!"

They wandered back and on the way they met Mira.

"Where are your parents?" asked Truphena.

"I had a letter this afternoon to say that they could not come, because father is away and mother is expecting the new baby soon and didn't feel she could manage the journey."

Mira was clearly very lonely and disappointed. "Come and join us," said Truphena, and introduced her to her mother and the rest of the family.

At that moment, a cousin of Truphena's appeared. "Hallo, Truphena," he said. "I heard that it was your Graduation Ceremony today and I thought I would come along and see you. You were just a tiny scrap when I stayed at your home the last time."

Truphena did not really remember him, but her mother said he was her sister's eldest son. She introduced him to Mira and they started talking.

Murimi came across to the party and brought his mother, who had only just arrived. She had missed the last bus the night before, but had managed to find someone to take her to Lakimu. She was very proud of her son.

There was a great crowd for tea and everyone was in a gay mood. At last it was time for the guests to go home and, quite soon, Truphena found herself alone with Murimi. "Come for a walk before supper," he pleaded.

Somehow she knew that this was, for her and Murimi, a farewell occasion.

They walked down to the river, where they had spent so many happy hours, and sat down on a large rock, overlooking the rushing waters. Neither spoke.

Truphena felt a great peace come over her and she leaned against Murimi. He put his arm round her shoulders. "Come with me, Truphena," he said softly. "You will be happy as my wife. We can do great things together for our people."

Truphena closed her eyes. For no apparent reason, the face of the pilot who had flown her and Eleeja to the city hospital formed a clear image in her mind.

They sat perfectly still for a long time.

"I am sorry, Murimi," she said at last, "but I cannot marry you. Please do not ask my reasons, because I find them difficult to express. In a way, I love you, but...," she paused for a moment, "not quite enough."

Without a word, Murimi stood up. He took hold of Truphena's hands and drew her towards him. He kissed her gently. "Good-bye, my darling," was all he said.

Slowly, they walked back to the hospital.

* * * *

It was six weeks after the Graduation Ceremony and Murimi was leaving for Takima. He had worked for three months with the doctor in the Out-Patient's Department and was now ready to start his own dispensary.

Truphena went down to the bus-stop to see him off. They had little to say. As the bus came lumbering round the corner, Murimi turned and gave her one last kiss. She did not resist.

"I shall often think of you," he said.

"I shall think of you too," she replied.

The bus stopped and he climbed on. "Good-bye," he said.

"Good luck," she called, as she watched the bus roll away into the distance.

Her heart was heavy as she turned and walked back to the hospital and a momentary doubt came into her mind. She ran quickly to the Nurses' Home and changed into her uniform. She was just in time for duty. She had been alloted to the Surgical Ward and was soon to start as a 'theatre nurse'.

"Good morning, Nurse," said Sister, as soon as she arrived on the ward. "Put the screens round Mr. Odede and prepare him for his operation; then take Mr. Juma for his X-ray ..."

As Truphena became part of the busy life of the ward, she knew she had made the right decision.

Glossary of Technical Terms

Anaesthetic	Substance used to stop patient feeling pain during an operation either by putting him to sleep or by numbing the area.
Autoclave	Apparatus rather like a modern oven in which steam is put through at great pressure in order to kill germs. Used for cotton wool, towels, gowns etc. which cannot be sterilized by boiling.
Bed-bath	(sometimes called blanket-bath). A nurse gives a bed-bath when she washes a patient all over while he is lying on the bed because he is not allowed to be moved.
Blood-pressure	Force by which blood is circulated around body —this can be measured and changes with illness.
Cylinder	Round metal or glass container used to hold liquids, or bandages, cottonwool, etc.
Disinfectant	Liquid or powder used to kill or prevent germs.
Dressing	Pads, bandages etc. used on an injury or after an operation. To dress a wound is to put on clean pads and bandages.

Infectious disease	Illness that can easily be passed on to others.
Injection	Passing liquid medicine into the body through a needle attached to a syringe.
Inoculation	An injection of weakened or dead germs of a particular disease. It prevents a serious attack caused by the same germs.
Feeding-cup	Cup with long spout with which a nurse can feed a patient who cannot sit up.
Forceps	Blunt type of "scissors", long or short, used during operations and also when dressing wounds in order to pick up things without touching them by hand.
Gloves -rubber	Gloves made of very thin rubber worn by doctors and nurses at operations and also when dressing wounds, preparing patients for operations and sometimes when examining patients.
Gown	Long overall, tied with tapes at the back, worn over usual clothes by doctors and nurses during operations, and at other times when it is essential to be absolutely clean.
Hospital corners	A method of folding sheets and blankets at the corners of the bed so that they always look neat and tidy.

House Surgeon	Usually young, newly-qualified doctor who is doing a concentrated 7-months' course of surgery in a hospital. He lives in and is constantly 'on call'.
Mackintosh, (rubber, rubber-sheet)	Piece of rubber (or plastic) put between under-blanket and sheet to save mattress from becoming soiled.
Mask	There are two types of masks which are mentioned. One is made of thin cloth, with four strings to tie at the back of the head and is worn by doctors and nurses in operating theatres, when handling newborn babies, when dressing a wound or when they are working in a hospital while they have a cold. This sort of mask is used to prevent infection. The second type of mask is made of rubber and is placed over a patient's face when he is given anaesthetic before an operation.
Matron	A senior nurse who is responsible for the domestic affairs and nursing staff of a hospital.
Medical Ward	Section of a hospital for patients who need nursing care and medicine but do not need an operation.
Oxygen	A gas which is found in the air. In its pure form it is given to patients who have difficulty in breathing.

Oxygen Cylinders	Metal containers which hold oxygen.
Physician	A Doctor who specializes in diseases requiring medical, not surgical, treatment.
Pneumonia	A serious illness which causes swelling in the lining of the lungs and makes for difficulty in breathing.
Rubber, rubber sheet	—See *Mackintosh*.
Rubber ring	Round tube made of soft rubber which can be blown up to make in air cushion. Used to rest limbs and parts of body which might become sore through being in contact with the bed for a long time.
Screen	Folding curtained frame, often on wheels, which is used to put round patient's bed when he needs privacy.
Sister	A qualified nurse who is above Staff Nurses, but under Matron. Usually a Sister is in charge of each ward.
Skeleton	The bone framework of a human or animal. For teaching purposes a skeleton is strung together in the same way as it would be in life.

Sluice	Small room usually attached to each ward, where articles such as rubbers, bed-pans etc. used on the wards are washed out. To sluice is to wash out by running plenty of water through.
Specialist	Doctor who specializes in one particular branch of medical work — e.g. Heart Specialist. Usually has high qualifications.
Staff Nurse	Qualified nurse on permanent staff of hospital who takes over when Sister is off duty.
Sterile	Free from germs.
Sterilize	To make an article free from germs by applying heat.
Sterilizer	An apparatus of stainless steel used for boiling instruments.
Stretcher	Two poles with strong cloth in between used as bed for carrying sick or injured patients.
Surgeon	Doctor who performs operations.
Syringe	A glass or plastic tube fitted with a 'pusher' and a hollow needle. Liquid is drawn into the tube by pulling the 'pusher' and can then be pushed out through a needle for giving injections.

Temperature	The heat of the body varies greatly with illness. Normal body temperature is 37 degrees centigrade.
Ward	Long room with a number of beds. In each ward there are different types of patients, e.g. Medical Ward, Surgical Ward. A side ward is a single room, often attached to the main ward, where seriously ill or special patients can be nursed.
Wound	An injury to the body where the skin is cut; also used to describe the cut made by a Surgeon when he operates.

Published by Phoenix Publishers Ltd., Mellow Heights, Ngara Road, P. O. Box 30474-00100 and printed by Ramco Printing Works Ltd. Mombasa Road, P.O. Box 27750 - 00506, Nairobi, Kenya.